Split Second

I pulled the bike over to let a car pass, then realised that it was slowing down alongside me. Out of the passenger seat, a man was waving me down.

He got out of the car, smiling slightly. I stood behind my bike as he came towards me, wondering if I should fling it towards him and run. He just stared.

There was a definite moment when we sized each other up, as if a fight were on the cards. Just when I was getting sick of this stupid staring-out, he grabbed my wrist. I tried to turn it away from him, but put myself neatly into a half-nelson instead. I shouted with pain, but I couldn't get free. What was going to happen now?

Also available in Lions

The Chronicles of Prydain *Lloyd Alexander*
Behind the Attic Wall *Sylvia Cassedy*
Goodbye and Keep Cold *Jenny Davis*
There Will be a Next Time *Tony Drake*
Julia's Mending *Kathy Lynn Emerson*
The Girls in the Velvet Frame *Adèle Geras*
The Shirt Off a Hanged Man's Back *Dennis Hamley*
Gillyflower *Ellen Howard*
The Girls' Gang *Rose Impey*
Harold and Bella, Jammy and Me *Robert Leeson*
Rabble Starkey *Lois Lowry*
The Size Spies *Jan Needle*
The Hand-Me-Down Kid *Francine Pascal*
The Secret of the Indian *Lynne Reid Banks*
Miriam *Iris Rosofsky*

Nick Baker

Split Second

LIONS

First published in Great Britain by
HarperCollins Publishers Ltd, 1989
First published in Lions 1991

Lions is an imprint of
the Children's Division, part of
HarperCollins Publishers Ltd,
77-85 Fulham Palace Road, London W6 8JB

Printed and bound in Great Britain by
HarperCollinsManufacturing, Glasgow

For Sukey

1

The man behind the counter in the greasy café is staring at me. I've been in here for an hour now, and only had one Coke. While I sit, George feels further and further away. And I feel more and more tired. Mustn't, mustn't, *mustn't* go to sleep. Should I ask the man for another Coke, then pretend I've lost my money? He doesn't look the understanding type. But I've got to get to George. I'm not even sure if I can stand up any more. And what if George dies? He can't. He mustn't.

That last night, just before I went to sleep in the park, I tried hard to remember how my mum explained my dad's death to me. It was nearly eight years ago. I was eight.

I remember sitting on that old browny coloured sofa and pulling at a strand of the fabric of it, not wanting to listen. It was an accident, she told me, where Dad worked. He was a famous scientist, and something had gone wrong. I remember being confused, thinking of scientists as grey-haired men with moustaches and white coats in laboratories full of bubbling bottles and tubes.

Did my dad have a moustache? I can't remember without looking at the photograph, the only one there is of him, sitting at a desk with another man I didn't know. He looked younger than Dad, and they're both smiling, as if they were really proud of something. I'm sure I recognize that man, but I'm not sure where from. There's something about that photograph that I've always hated. I don't know why, because I loved my dad, as far as I can remember.

That week I didn't have to go to school. I went to stay with my Aunty Laurel and my cousin James, who was two. He hit me over the head with a small hammer he had in one of those stupid knock-in-the-peg games little kids have. My head started to bleed and Aunty Laurel went mad at him.

At the end of the week my mum picked me up and I think that's when we moved into this house, in a different town, far away from where we used to live with Dad. I went to a new school, and we had a new car and suddenly, it seemed everything was new and different. In the excitement, my dad seemed to fade away into the background. I think we were much richer than before and when I got my first bike for my ninth birthday, I felt it was like a new, fresh start.

I was fourteen the first time it happened. I remember this much more clearly, every single detail has stayed with me. It was a Wednesday, I'd been playing football after school, it was winter.

I'd had beefburgers and a baked potato for my supper, it was eight o'clock and my mum was ironing in the kitchen. I remember the swish of the iron and the clean, steamy smell coming through the door into the living room. I was glued to the television, lying in the armchair, my legs dangling carelessly over one side. I was, as they say, "transfixed". Glued, goggle-eyed to the screen. The programme was one of those deep-sea diving expeditions which showed you all sorts of weird fish.

Spiky, fat ones. Green, see-through ones. Ones which didn't look like fish, but stones, lying on the sea bed sucking in water. Bubbly noises and weird music. Every so often a man's voice, telling you about the fish. Mesmeric is the word. Or hypnotic.

As the programme went on, I became more and more aware that I wanted to have a pee. Typical. Just when there's something good on, the old bladder starts to take over. Perhaps it was all that water. I didn't want to miss any of the programme, but I needed to go.

Then, the thought. One tiny little thought that changed my life and could have changed the world too, if they hadn't caught up with me. Wouldn't it be great if I could go, and sort of stay at the same . . .

I blinked, feeling that during the blink I'd fallen asleep.

Then I got up to go to the loo . . .

I got as far as about halfway across the carpet and then, I don't know why, I looked back at the armchair. And there I was. Still. I turned, almost calmly, and walked towards the chair. It was me in the chair and me walking towards the chair.

And then me reaching out to the other me, still glued to the TV and the fish and then me touching the hand and then sort of trying to stand up and get out of the chair and then finding I couldn't because I was so heavy and falling . . .

All in the space of perhaps five, maybe ten seconds. The next thing I knew, my mum was sort of leaning me against a chair and saying "What happened?" What happened? I'd split for the first time.

Hospitals, doctors, nurses, Aunty Laurel, Mum, more doctors, tests, sticking things in my arm, to my chest, to my head. The next week went in a sort of blur. I was ambulanced to the local hospital where attention was poured on me. I felt exhausted, as if I'd done the school cross-country twice. All the while I was being probed I was trying to sort out what had happened to me, trying to make it safe.

I had fainted, I told myself dimly between proddings and pokings, and while I was unconscious I had dreamed what had happened. It was my fertile imagination working overtime. But I wasn't supposed to have a fertile imagination – almost all my compositions came back marked "uninspiring", "lacking development" and so on.

Naturally I told the quiet-voiced, plain-clothes psychiatrist who came to talk to me in the ghastly children's ward nothing of the split. I wasn't sure any longer what had happened myself.

"Nervous exhaustion and stress" and some stuff I didn't understand about my father and his death was eventually diagnosed. I'd have been happy enough to go along with this and accept the two months off school prescribed as treatment, together with increased doses of mumsiness from my otherwise level-headed mother, but for one thing. As I regained my strength, sitting around the house or going for short but nevertheless boring walks through the park, I began to remember the feeling I had, the thought, just before the split.

It began to get much clearer. The fish, the woozy feeling and more and more the desire to be in two places at once, in fact the whole experience

11

began to seem clearer. What was frightening was the feeling that I could do it again. I didn't know whether I wanted to or not.

I certainly knew that I couldn't tell anyone about it. I imagined telling Dr McPherson, our doddery old GP whose hands shook:

"Well, actually, Doc, the whole thing can be put down to the fact that I can make myself into two people whenever I feel like it", and being carried off to the funny farm while Mum looked on, weeping.

The other thing was that I felt guilty about it, as if splitting into two was the sort of thing to be ashamed of, like burping in public or making a rude noise in assembly.

But the more I thought about it, the more I felt I could do it again. I was scared all right, but only scared about being found out, not about what it would do to me physically. And there were still lots of questions to be answered, like:

1 When I split for the first time did my clothes split as well? I remember the me that was left on the sofa was clothed, but was the one in the middle of the living room?

2 How long could I do it for? The whole thing lasted a couple of seconds the first time. If I tried to remain split for longer, what would happen to the me I'd split from, the one that didn't move? I had horrible visions of the first me dying and the second me having to bury the body before

anyone found out. Surely this would be a crime, something like suicide.

3 Really this should be number one. WHY WAS THIS HAPPENING TO ME?

The only way to answer 1 and 2, of course, was to try an experiment. I was due to return to school in the next couple of days, and I had to plan it carefully. In bed, last thing at night, was the answer, after I'd heard Mum go to bed. She'd stay up, squeezing the television dry of the last current affairs programme and boring old vicar and weather forecast.

It was only then that I realized how lonely she must have been. Even when Dad was alive, she spent a lot of time alone in the old house because of his work, and I suppose I was always too busy being a kid, preoccupied with bikes and toys and stuff to be any real company. By this time she'd got herself some sort of part-time job but she never really saw anybody, just me.

Anyway, it got to the stage where I didn't dare put it off. On the last night before I went back to school after my long "illness", I had to know. I know what decided me. I'd been away about three months and then Mum got a letter from school saying they thought it would be better if I did the whole school year again the following year, as I'd missed some important work. Cheek!

So maybe it was partly rebellion. That night me and Mum watched a load of old crap on TV and at ten, as usual, I was told to go to bed.

I'd thought things out quite carefully, pretending to go to sleep as soon as I got to bed, so when Mum came up to say goodnight finally she wouldn't come back into my room. For the first time ever I was thankful I didn't have any brothers and sisters.

I could hear the TV droning on downstairs, looking at the clock every half hour, only to find that no more than five minutes had passed. Sleep was, of course, out of the question. Supposing I fell asleep during the split? I'd had this awful thought that afternoon, of my mum waking me for school the next day and finding, for the first time in eleven years, that she was the mother of twins, but that only one of them could move about and talk.

I'd prepared for this by making myself a Thermos full of black coffee with loads of sugar in it, to keep me awake and give me energy. I'd also put a spare pair of pyjamas on the chair, just in case the second me did turn out to be naked.

After about three months' wait, swigging at the coffee and staring at the luminous hands of the alarm clock, I heard the telltale sounds of the TV being switched off, followed by bathroom noises, followed by the sound of my mum's bedroom door shutting. Now or never.

All right. More details needed. Of course, I

should have explained things better. Said more about my dad, my mum, being a kid. Only George is in hospital and I'm here and what if they pull the plug? Or worse still, what if they find me? I've got to get back to George, but how?

Never mind, some details to be getting on with. Name: Gordon Watts. Only child of Margaret and Harrison Watts. Margaret Watts: widow. Age: thirty-nine I think. Part-time secretary in estate agent in St Albans. Moved to Beckford, boring town on northern outskirts of London four years ago, from Watford, where we lived before and where father, Harrison Watts, worked, at something called Department of the Environment Physical Research Project. Age at death: forty.

I know how hard it always was for Mum to talk about him. How painful it was. She wanted me to have a sense of him because he died when I was so young. When I was eleven or twelve, it didn't seem to mean much, in fact I sometimes wished she would stop. Like, when they told me that I had to do the third year again.

It was a big show up, really embarrassing, and all Mum could do was say how important my education was, going on about how clever, no, brilliant, Dad was and how young he was to have got so far. What did that have to do with me? Anyway, I always thought forty was old, but I never said.

My recollections of him are strictly kids' stuff. Him bringing home presents and us going to the park to feed the ducks or play football. But mostly of him working all the time, always at the Project because he couldn't bring anything home. And sometimes men coming to the house, old men with corny scientist-type German accents and funny suits. Or quiet, thin men who, when confronted with an ordinary child of seven or eight, didn't quite know how to react. And one neither corny-German nor thin and quiet, but quite ordinary looking – he could have been a milkman or a prime minister. I think I only met him about once or twice, but I always remember laughing to myself because his name was Edward, and I had a toy pig – a sort of teddy pig called Edward.

Once, when we were left alone together in the sitting room while the Sunday lunch was being prepared and the telly was on for my amusement, Edward took me by the shoulders, looked into my face and said: "Your father is a great man. It's the only word to describe him."

All I felt was embarrassment. Was he the man in the photograph with my father, that still stands on the shelf at home? I can't remember. I wish I could.

And me? Me now? Or, to be more exact, before the business with George? I was ordinary. I wanted to be ordinary. I knew my mum was clever, and my father was A Great Man and by some magical rule that means that I have to be clever too, but I wasn't. I was sort of good at some things and sort of not very good at others. All my school reports used to say things like "fair" or "average" or "able, but must take more care" or "could be fairly careful if he wasn't so averagely able" or "averagely able of being capably fair, but could be more careful". They used to say that until my illness, of course.

All crap. I was the kid at the back, the one who's tall for his age, the one whose name the teacher leaves until last to learn. With other kids I was the one in the background, watching. It's how I wanted to be.

It was only natural, I suppose, that my mum was for ever worried about me. Worried about the absence of signs of Dad-like budding genius, I expect. She came to school once or twice. Spoke to the headmaster.

Got on at me, in a fairly tactful sort of way I suppose, to work a bit harder. Read books and stuff. Have friends over. Get interested in things. I did for a while, even found I enjoyed it in an odd sort of way. But after that first split in front of the television that night there was only one thing that I was really interested in.

I lay in bed, hardly daring to breathe. I knew what feelings I needed to have in order to make the split, and for one moment I felt that I wasn't going to be able to do it again – that I'd imagined it, or that it was a flash in the pan. Then, calmly, I remembered. The fish, the pleasant, relaxed feeling, the want to . . .

I suddenly found a new meaning for the words split second. Blink. In that second, it had happened. I was standing, my back to my bed, in the middle of the room. I knew that I had no clothes on and I knew that if I turned round I'd see the other me lying in bed. A spooky feeling, half pleasure, half fear ran down my spine. I dared myself to turn, and there, dimly lit by the yellowy street lamp outside, he was.

I had to say "he" because the moment I saw him I realized that we were two people. "He" was lying in my bed, seemingly asleep, eyes closed. I turned my back again, determined to make sure that it was real, not a dream.

I knew that it was. Real, I mean. "He" or I, it was impossible to work out, was standing in the middle of the bedroom, with no clothes on. So, the next thing to do, I felt, was get dressed. Without looking back at "him". I got into the other pyjamas I'd prepared, (blue, this time – "his" were red) put them on, fumbling with buttons like a five-year-old, then turned again.

"He" was still there, unmoving except for the slight breathing movements of an ordinary fourteen-year-old, asleep in bed.

George. I called him George for no good

reason – perhaps because it was the same initial as mine, perhaps for a joke, I don't know.

Cautiously I walked towards the bed, looked closer. Weird! Like when you see yourself on videotape for the first time and you know that it's you you're watching, but somehow it's not the same you you imagined yourself to be.

Impossible to describe, the feeling I had. So that's what I look like, I thought. Sort of slightly smaller but slightly older than the me I saw every morning in the mirror. But apart from that, exactly the same. The same blond hair, eyebrows, shape of the chin, tiny pimple on cheek. Same hands, fingernails chewed, folded peacefully on top of the covers, in the way I always slept. Eyes closed. They'd be the same colour, I was sure. The more I got used to it the more fascinated I was to see. But I seemed to know, instinctively, I suppose, that if I touched "him" – sorry, if I touched GEORGE – we'd become one person again.

And what, I can hear you asking, would happen to the pyjamas? I sat staring at George for a few minutes more. He didn't stir, neither did I. Then nothing.

I don't remember touching George, no jolt as we became boring old Gordon Watts again. But when I awoke, early the next morning, I was aware, like when you wake up for the first time

19

in a strange bed, of something different. That I felt too warm and sort of uncomfortably twisted. I looked down at myself (should I say ourself? No, too complicated) and saw that I was wearing two pairs of pyjamas, blue over the top of red. And the blue ones were buttoned up wrongly as if in haste. Proof.

I looked at the clock, wondering if there was time to try again before Mum woke up. Seven, nearly. No time. And it was school today. How was I going to concentrate on anything?

I got up, carefully folded and replaced the blue pyjamas, then got back into bed. "How? Why? What?" was what I should have been thinking, like now. Looking back I realize how young, how immature I was.

What I'm thinking now is, "How can I get back to George?"

I can hardly drink the Coke (sugar for energy, remember?) in front of me. I'm exhausted, asleep nearly. And I know that if I do fall asleep, it's curtains for George.

2

The day after the incident with the pyjamas, I went back to school. Sitting (as usual) at the back of the class, I could think of nothing else but the split and about what I could do with it. Naturally, I decided not to tell anybody. Even then, I didn't want to be regarded as a freak, a circus act or a scientific curiosity. I'd had enough of questions and proddings in the hospital after the first time.

I was like a kid who'd found out what his birthday present was three weeks before his birthday. I couldn't boast about it to anybody, all I could do was play with it in secret, then replace it, wrapped up again on top of my mum's wardrobe.

For the next couple of weeks, every night, I did nothing but experiment, splitting and "unsplitting" again and again until I was so tired I collapsed into a dead sleep. The first thing I tried was to split standing up, to see if George

21

would fall over. He didn't, he just stood there, statue-like, eyes open, breathing lightly and blinking every so often. If I touched him, or even his clothes, we'd unsplit and I'd need five minutes to recover.

Gradually I became more confident, splitting and recovering with more and more ease. I got up the courage to leave the room for a moment. "He" was still there when I got back. In the space of a fortnight, my life turned upside down.

Dear Claire Rayner,
I'm fourteen and a half years old, and although I have one mind, I have two bodies. Sometimes. What should I do?
       Gordon

Dear Gordon,
Don't worry, because lots of boys of your age suffer from the problem of having two bodies. Look on the bright side! You can play table tennis by yourself, and chess, and you can tidy your bedroom in no time at all. The main thing is not to feel too self-conscious, and always carry a spare set of clothes, so that if you do split in the middle of the high street, you can get your clothes on before the cops come . . .
      Claire Rayner

My worst problem, of course, was that I could

tell nobody. Not a soul. It was the worst sort of secret because it was impossible to share. I've always experienced a sort of sense of danger about splitting – that it would really kill me in the end. And I do want someone to know. I just don't want to be there when they find out.

So, on with the story.

During that first two weeks, alone and splitting, I could think of nothing else. My teachers started to complain that I looked tired, lacked interest, couldn't be bothered. It was true. Roman roads, *White Fang* and pottery held no interest for me.

For English homework, once, I wrote the story of me splitting, then tore it up on the way to school and got into trouble.

"Gordon, what's happening to you?" whined Miss Peters in a Play School voice. "I thought you were such a bright boy." She thought nothing of the sort, but you have to give her credit for trying to get through to me.

My mum started to moan too, and started to go on about "adolescence" and how much I cost to feed. She made me sound like a zoo animal. Actually, I was eating a lot. I couldn't control my hunger. I'd have biscuits and stuff when I got back from school, mooch around in the kitchen for my mum to throw me scraps while she was making tea. Then I'd have tea. And seconds. Then I'd go and do my homework and split a bit. Then I'd watch TV, feeling tired, and eat a sandwich, a bowl of cereal or a few pounds of biscuits.

Splitting was brilliant. For a start, it wasn't long before I could get George to move, and then to move myself at the same time. All a matter of coordination, like riding a bike. I could also "let" George wander about, absentmindedly, without having to think much about what he was doing. Not that he did much. Just wandered absentmindedly.

I'll never forget the first time I heard him speak. I thought he never would, but it was quite easy to make him.

"Hello, George," I said to him.

"Hello, George," he said back to me in a voice that sounded like me on tape. Then we both fell about laughing, touched accidentally, joined again and fell over in a tangle of clothes.

Another discovery: when we were out of each other's sight, I could, if I wanted to, see with George's eyes. A sort of "split screen" effect. I could see both where I was and where George was at the same time, with a bit of concentration.

The first great experiment was to send George downstairs to see whether Mum would notice the difference. He wandered downstairs, me guiding him telepathically towards the kitchen.

Mum looked at George without curiosity. Meanwhile, George stared at Mum for any signal that she suspected anything. Nothing.

I found that while George was in the kitchen, filching raw carrots, I could occupy my mind with something else – staring out of the window, practising my eleven times table, even doing a bit of reading. George seemed perfectly OK.

"Gordon!" Twelve elevens are . . . I was jerked to my (or rather George's) senses. At first I thought that it was Mum calling me from downstairs. Then I realized, "tuning in" to George, that I'd been concentrating too hard on twelve elevens, and George was staring absentmindedly at the cooker switch.

Nothing suspicious about that. I'd earned a reputation for being a dreamer since the splitting had started.

"Are you listening to me?"

"Yes."

"What did I just say?"

"Something about laying the table," George guessed, with my help.

"What's the matter with you?" she asked, not really wanting an answer. "They all used to say how you took after your father, how you'd inherit his brains, follow in his foot . . ."

Uh oh. Mention of my father had sent my mind back to the photograph on the mantelpiece (why did I hate it so much?) and left poor old George's mind high and dry, apparently transfixed by a small piece of carrot.

Mum's face started to crumple. She had a

characteristic way of biting her lip before crying, a signal I learnt about when she mourned my father. Even an eight-year-old can see the signs.

"I'm worried about you, Gordon," she said, tremulously. "You're not doing anything you . . ."

Shouldn't? Taking drugs? Befriending loony strangers? Shoplifting? Sticking aerosol bottles up my nose and pressing the button? Raiding the sherry bottle? Jamming my little fingers into the electric sockets? No, Mum. Something far, far worse. Or better.

Fun? It was brilliant, the time I had that summer, once George and I had got the splitting sorted out. I – I must keep to calling myself I because there's only one of me. George became a sort of shadow of me, and although he had no "character" of his own, if you'd met him at that time you'd think that this was a pleasant thicko. I'd deliberately leave him with a smile on his face, a sort of dreamy smile that said nothing, while I got up to all sorts.

But before I could get up to anything, we had to experiment, and the house wasn't the place to do it. So that summer, it was off to the woods, tracksuited (for ease of splitting – with George in sports gear inside the tracksuit) and with a big, energy-giving picnic.

"I don't know where you put it all," my mum smiled thinly as I asked for an extra sandwich or drink or something. "There's enough there for two."

The actual splitting became easier and easier, and so did the control of George. We'd go for a walk in the woods, and I'd move further and further away from him, as if he was on a sort of autopilot. Meanwhile, I could concentrate quite well. At first, he'd bump into things, bits of trees would hit him in the face, or if I was doing something particularly interesting, he'd stop altogether through lack of concentration. Gradually our range grew. As we got used to splitting, we found we could increase the distance between us without feeling that telltale tiredness.

I'll always remember the first time George actually met a stranger. We were maybe fifty metres apart, George trudging automatically through the scrubby woodland, a hot summer day, me "tracking" him at a distance, occasionally taking a look at what he was looking at but for the main part making him get on with a "task" without too much effort from me. Picking up stones, or something. One thing about old George, he never got bored.

Anyway, in the middle of the wood, I came across an old car. God knows how it had got there – it was about a mile from the nearest road and it had obviously been dumped quite recently. I was doing a typical little boy "I wonder if I could get it started" fantasy in my head, forgetting about George altogether.

Suddenly I became aware of this loud voice. "The boy's obviously daft. Leave him be."

Then another one. "Damn rude, I call it. We only asked him which way it was to the road."

For a split second, I was terrified. Thought I was being haunted. It made the car seem sort of spooky. Then I realized, and brought George to his senses (or should I say mine) and saw, through his eyes, a couple of OAPs staring at him. Of course, George was just grinning like a friendly fool, not paying them the slightest bit of attention, like a mad person from a documentary on BBC 2.

Not wanting to dispel the old couple's belief that George was a moron, I made him point vaguely towards the road, and watched them trail off, shaking their heads sympathetically. Then I realized how useful George could be. He could be a servant, a friend, and a plaything. But he'd need a lot more training.

Why did I not think more about why this was happening? Look in library books, they're always telling us at school. Find out why things happen for yourself. Well, part of the reason was that I just didn't have time. During that summer the routine was get into two tracksuits (one inside the other), grab as much food as possible, make a dash for the woods and start experimenting. And playing.

I'd tell Mum that I was going with mates and she seemed quite happy. But why did I not link splitting and my old dead dad? (That's right, I've got no respect for the dead. Specially when they're my dad and they keep secrets from me.)

Maybe I realized in the back of my mind that he was at the bottom of the mystery. Mum was only too willing to tell me how brilliant he was, but when it came to details about his work, she didn't seem to know much, or didn't want to say. The truth was that I was far more interested in playing my new game than working out how I'd learned the rules.

No use looking elsewhere. I was hardly likely to find the answer in a library book, was I?

The other incident from that summer that sticks in my mind (half because it was so funny and half because it was so dangerous) happened in a shop. Discrimination, I called it. I was on the way to the bit of wood where George and I could be more or less undisturbed. I was wearing two tracksuits, one inside the other. This became a kind of uniform, by the way. I'd find a secluded spot, split, George would be naked and I'd take off the outer suit and he'd put it on post haste. That morning I'd had no breakfast for some reason, and had stopped at the village shop where I used to get off the bus from Beckford. All right, what I did could have caused the lady in the shop to die from a heart attack, but at fourteen you don't worry too much about little details like that.

I was waiting behind some commuter who was buying a newspaper. I'd picked a Mars Bar from the shelf and had my money ready. Just as the first bloke paid, another came in, picked up a paper, and the lady behind the counter ignored me, my Mars and my money and started wazzing on to this bloke about the weather. Then some woman came in and pushed in front of me. Typical village stuff. Because they all knew each other, they automatically elbowed me, not only because I was a stranger but also because I was a kid.

And of course, this far from ordinary kid was anxious to get the calories down his neck and leg it to the woods. So when all the Archers-style nattering had finished, and the shop was empty but for me, the old boot behind the counter was surprised to see that I'd eaten one Mars Bar, left the wrapper neatly on the counter and was half way into my second.

"Why, you young . . . how dare you come into my shop and . . ."

"I was going to pay," I protested. "You just never gave me a chance!"

"That's theft!" wailed boot features, ignoring me.

"No it isn't!"

It was no good arguing. She already had her hand on the phone under the counter.

Anger, mad bravery and high calorie injection (I can really feel it, you know, like looking at the petrol gauge in a car) combined. Smiling sweetly and still holding out my money, I split, still chomping. George appeared immediately, naked as the day I was born, also chomping and offering, but with nothing in his mouth or his hand.

Boot's jaw dropped. She looked at us both, moving her head like a tennis umpire. Then, with a burst of crazy confidence, I did it again.

It was all logical, I realized. If George was a carbon copy of me then he could split too, it stood to reason.

There were now three of us. Identical triplets, two without a stitch. Then again.

"So sorry to have caused you any trouble," said the three nudists and me, with painful politeness.

Boot turned white and began to sway slightly. The phone fell out of her hand. She tried to say something, but all that came out was a weak gurgle. In that instant I realized how stupid and dangerous this was, and at the same time began to feel a bit weedy myself. So me and my new

31

brothers joined hands as if we were bowing at the end of a pantomime, joined up again so there was just me there (another faint gurgle from Doc Marten), put the money on the counter and made a hasty exit, never to return.

As soon as I got out I began to feel strange. Very tired, and a little frightened at myself. First, looking across at the other Georges was like looking at a very strange hall of mirrors. The fact they were naked made it worse, much more mad, like a nightmare.

Then I wondered what was happening to the woman in the shop. It must have been a horrible shock for her – a thousand times worse than what it was like for me. Like someone had slipped some weirdo drug into her tea without her knowing. And suppose she told someone? I felt worse. Shaken up and shivery.

Instead of going into the woods that day, I went straight home on the bus, shaken up a bit. I even went round to my mate Terry's house, because I wanted to feel "normal" for a bit.

But I'd learnt a lot from boot features. About the need to keep my secret and the danger to other people if I didn't. About the control of energy – knowing what my limits were and not blowing the whole power supply on one stupid, careless joke. And another lesson, more important than the first two – I started thinking about how to put my strange talent to good use.

3

But by then, it was getting near the end of the summer, and I realized that if I continued being distracted by splitting, then I'd be in more trouble. So when the first day of term came, I really made an effort. Got involved. No long experimental splits, no fooling around, just a lot of being normal and at school trying to understand French and physics.

And I did too. Understand French and physics. It all got quite interesting. For a while I was getting good marks, having a good time, and even making a few friends. Terry Stones was a laugh. So was Lee Wild. I realized that I'd missed a lot of this friends business over the last year, and I also realized how important it was both to me, and I suppose to George, but more importantly to Mum, that I get normal.

But I was always a bit distant from Lee and Terry. And although I was often a bit tempted to introduce them to George, I never did. You know when you're mucking about with your mates and everyone's trying to get everyone's attention by doing something really clever or dangerous or stupid, like climbing trees and pretending to fall out or being cheeky to people, I always wanted to then, but I realized I couldn't. Besides which, although Lee was always trying to be one of the lads, he was a bit of a weed at heart and I don't know whether he could have taken it.

Terry could have, maybe. He was a trustworthy type. But I suspected Lee was just a tiny bit thick (well, I knew, really, and I think he did too) and I thought that if he ever got to know he wouldn't be able to stop himself telling everyone else.

I started to grow too. Outwards. I was already quite tall for my age and suddenly I got quite broad and a bit taller. So did George, of course. And although I wasn't doing half the splitting I'd done the previous summer, I was still always hungry.

This seemed to delight my mum now. She was always feeding me up and smiling and saying how I reminded her more and more of my dad. She began to talk a bit more about him too. What he was like when they first met, and how he was so pleased with me when I was born, and stuff.

Not that it meant all that much to me. I suppose I'd half worked out that my peculiar talents were something to do with his secret job, but I couldn't work out what. Whenever the conversation between me and my mum did turn to Dad, I would always try and winkle out what he actually did, without much success. She'd pretend she didn't know. Maybe she really didn't.

January 5th was an important day. It was a year after my little "attack", when I learnt that I could split and had my fainting fit. I was booked in to have a check-up. Only the plain-clothes head shrinker that I saw in Beckford had moved to a hospital in London, so I had to go and see him there.

Out of the blue, my mum arranged that we'd go in the morning, and then we'd meet Lee and Terry at King's Cross and we'd all go out for lunch and then see the latest American sci-fi laser special effect space film.

Looking back, I think my mum thought I'd be a bit worried about the doctoring business, and the afternoon treat was to keep my mind off it. Actually, she was right about the hospital stuff. Not that I was scared of needles or anything. What worried me was that they'd somehow find out about big G.

By this time my twin bro had "learnt" a little more, but if you met him you'd think he was a dimwit. He could *just* read, very slowly, as long as I wasn't doing anything more complicated than, say, walking in a straight line.

He could talk independently of me – answer questions, talk on the phone, and so on, provided my mind wasn't too occupied and the questions were easy.

Put it this way. If *I*, as command module, was doing anything independently, he had the brain power of a five-year-old. The more I was doing, the less he could.

If I sat and did nothing he became me, more or less. And vice versa. Doing two things at a time was hard work – the more different they were, the more difficult it got. But gradually we learnt.

Hard to explain how. Like some cheapo computers. You know if you're using one to work something out or write something and you want to print out at the same time, then everything slows down. Gets laboured. Concentrate on one task and you're OK. In the back of my mind, I suppose, I was preparing for George's first day at school, by himself. That would be really something.

Christmas was still lurking messily about on the London streets on the day of the visit to the doctor. I got a tracksuit as a present – dead useful. I thought of buying something for George but I realized early on that it was important never to treat him as a separate person.

That day, Mum and me got up at the crack of dawn, her a bit apprehensive, I could tell, and also dressed up rather more than usual.

And as usual in hospitals, we're kept waiting about three days and finally they do all the stuff to me that hospitals are supposed to – stick wooden things down your throat to make sure that you can still puke in an emergency, check that you can blush properly by making you take all your clothes off and making you wee into a bottle, taking your blood, your pulse, your temperature, your blood pressure and all that.

Mum waited outside while all this was going on. I reckon she was doing it to impress on me that I was growing up and able to be humiliated on my own without her help.

Then I was put into this great big machine – a sort of hollow cylinder with loads of Dr Who-type knobs and dials and computer read-outs. I had a sudden desire, just for the hell of it, to split while I was inside, and for me and George to come out and say to the doc: "There must be something wrong with it, I went in by myself."

Then it was up to the hospital canteen for a cup of revolting tea and a Wagon Wheel. The sugar and the relief at thinking it was all over made me fancy another split, but of course with no spare clothes it was out of the question.

Anyway, it wasn't all over. Mum announced that we had to go across town to Harley Street for me to have more tests. This made me feel slightly worried. What would they discover that they hadn't already discovered from the hospital? Why was I being given all this medical attention? Did Mum know more than she pretended?

"Look, Gordon," she said to me earnestly as we got on the tube. "When you were ill that time, they did find something a little bit, well, unusual about you."

Uh oh. "How d'you mean, unusual?" I asked as innocently as I could.

"I don't understand the details myself. But it's nothing to worry about. They promised me that it wasn't dangerous, and that what they really wanted was to study you for some medical text-book. Something to do with the way your brain shows up on their equipment, that's all."

Oh, great, I thought. They know. They must do. What's going to happen to me? After all, I'm a freak. Freaks get put away. And God knows what sort of thing they might dream up to put my strange talent to work.

Like, supposing you're a spy, and you can split. You can be in one place while your double sits somewhere else, creating an alibi. What if they want to take a closer look at my brain? Whatever they're seeing on their machines will have grown over the past year, so they're likely to want to look closer.

Suppose they want to flip my head open like a

boiled egg, and get it out for a dig about – what happens then? As the tube reached Mornington Crescent, I felt sicker and sicker. Maybe I should confide in my mother, I thought. Maybe she knows already.

I decided not to tell anyone. Not to say anything. Keep it dark. If the mad scientist in Harley Street says to me "Can you split?" I'd pretend not to know a thing.

We arrived at the surgery, which was like a big old house. Without any waiting about staring at magazines, we were shown into a big sitting room with a desk in the middle. Behind the desk sat a man who looked your standard doctor type. Whether he was the man I'd seen a year earlier in hospital I don't recall. Glasses, suit, old-fashioned shirt and tie, fountain pen in hand, grey hair, slightly bushy eyebrows. He and another man were staring intently at some computer paper.

I had a feeling I'd seen the other man before. Maybe he was a doctor from my last "illness" too. When he looked up, though, I got the impression that he didn't want me to see him, or he didn't want to see me. I remember this clearly. He gave me one piercing look, dead suspicious, as if I was a mass murderer or something. Then he looked away, picked up a pile of papers and sort of bustled out, not saying anything or meeting my eye again. For some reason this freaked me out a bit. We sat down across the desk from the doctor. If my mum had suggested that she'd leave me and the doc together, I would have insisted that she stayed, no matter how babyish I might have seemed.

I could have skipped down those steps half an hour later. I could have run up to the policeman who happened to be passing and knocked his helmet off. What a relief. Grey-haired Dr Fowles turned out, of all things, to be another shrink. A trick cyclist. A mad doctor. Before I had time to ask, he explained why I was such an interesting case. He said that when they plugged my brain into the computer, the read-outs were unlike anything anyone's ever seen. There were two of everything.

I gulped. They *must* know, then. Dr Fowles started to go on about how it wasn't that unusual for people to be born with two hearts or four kidneys or ten stomachs or something, and I was just expecting the worst when he said:

"So, Gordon, apart from having the most peculiar brain patterns known to medical science, you appear perfectly normal. A picture of health, in fact. And what the boffins at the hospital have asked me to do is to check that you're not bonkers."

I smiled. I knew I wasn't bonkers, and I

thought it was quite funny that a psychiatrist should use such a stupid word. He smiled, too, suggested to my mum that she could wait outside and that we wouldn't be long.

Then he asked me loads of questions about myself, what I was interested in, whether I had friends, liked school, what I wanted to be when I grew up, all dead straightforward. The only dodgy one was whether I liked girls or not, which he asked me in a meaningful sort of way.

I looked embarrassed and looked at my shoes and muttered something like "they're all right", which seemed to be the right answer, because he smiled broadly, put away his pen, took off his glasses and stood up. It was all over. The most dramatic thing was that some doctor might want to write about me in a special magazine for brain specialists, but they wouldn't print my name.

He repeated all this to my mother in the hall, who also looked visibly relieved. And then we were in the street, and Mum said, "Let's look for a taxi" which was another treat because I'd never been in one before. When we finally found one and got in, I saw that she was crying. I gave her a hug and found that I was nearly crying too. Don't know why. We soon had to wipe our eyes, though, because we were dead near King's Cross, and we knew that Terry and Lee would be waiting for us, ready for our post-Christmas, post-psychiatrist treat.

It was a good afternoon, made even better by the relief I felt. My secret was still intact. Over a sandwich and a Coke, Terry and Lee kept up their usual double act of stupid jokes and hysterical laughter. They were dead polite and nice to my mum which was good, because she didn't know them that well.

As we set off on the tube again for the cinema, Lee doing his alien life in Beckford impersonation in preparation for the film, I felt really happy. We were like a family for the day. For a moment I even wished my dad could have been there.

The funny thing about all these science fiction films is that you *know* they're not true, yet you always believe them.

We walked across the centre of London, me forgetting all about the morning. Until, that is, we reached this big square place with lots of posh shops and lots of tourists. There was a little crowd, shuffling with cold, watching this sort of skiffle band who were busking. We watched for a minute too, standing among the Japanese cameras and American accents, our breath cloudy in the cold air. Lee and Terry started this little double act of their own, pretending to play guitars and stuff. Then the buskers finished and my life changed again.

Onto the makeshift stage strolled a bloke of about twenty – a sort of hippy-looking bloke, with a big hat and baggy dungarees. From out of his dungarees, he took some fruit. An apple, an orange and a banana. He started juggling.

Lee got very excited about this.

"I can juggle with three things – easy!" he said, his eyes glued on the hippy. "Easy!"

Hippy started to juggle, all the time keeping up this funny very fast talk about fruit being good for you. Then, still juggling, be began to eat the apple. Every time it went past his left hand, he took a bite. Soon he was juggling with just a core.

"Wicked," breathed Lee.

And it was. Soon the hippy had finished the apple, core and all, and got out a bread roll and an egg. Now he was juggling with roll, banana, orange and egg, eating the banana bit by bit and dropping the skin on the floor.

"Betya he slips!" yelled Lee, like a kid at a pantomime.

Hippy heard him. "Don't give the game away, man!" he yelled back. At the same time he was getting out one of those squeezy sauce bottles that look just like huge tomatoes. Still juggling, he made a sandwich out of the roll, the sauce and the egg, which was still in its shell. Then he started eating it. He got a big salt container out, started to pretend to put salt on the sandwich; it was all getting too fast.

You couldn't really make out what was going on. And he began to lurch about, losing control, and of course, he did slip on the banana skin, but as he did that, he sort of flung everything up into the air and then, sitting on his backside he caught it all – sandwich, sauce bottle, salt, orange.

Mucho applause. People who didn't want to part with their money drifted away, and he ran about with his hat, collecting cash. By the time he got to us he must have had about ten quid in change. I had a brilliant idea.

It turned out that Lee was telling the truth when he said he could juggle with three things. Not very well, but not badly. For the rest of the Christmas holidays, I got him to teach me. The trick is . . . well, never mind what the trick is, but by the time we went back to school, what with practising and all, I could do it just as well as Lee. And so, of course, could George.

Teaching George to read opened my eyes to the change that had come over me. I had vowed never to treat him as a separate person, but I realized that without certain abilities, George would be more of a problem than an asset.

And that meant being able to do certain things. So far he could wander about, "see" things and keep out of physical trouble. He couldn't hold a proper conversation with anyone, though. Or work anything out for himself. He was almost completely without processing power. So, one day when I was home early from school and my mum was still at work, I started to "teach" George to read and write properly.

"Right, George," I said after we'd split. "You're going to learn a couple of things."

"OK," he said, and grinned.

It was ridiculous, really. Like talking to yourself and looking in a mirror. But a plan was forming in my mind – a plan that would leave George at school while I investigated London a bit more. So, George had to learn.

"Sorry, George, old boy. You've got to learn."

"I suppose I have."

We both giggled, embarrassed.

Then an experiment. I gave George a pen to hold, and a piece of paper. Then I took pen and paper myself. The idea was for us *both* to write our names down at once, One, two three go.

Mine was fine. George's looked like this:

George looked up and scowled. So did I. This was not going to be easy. We tried reading. I found the simplest thing I could – a kids' book about pirates that I'd read years ago. We both looked at it together. It was fine.

We could both read the same thing at once, no problem.

"No problem," said George, and smiled.

I'd have to watch this, I thought. Let George have too much personality and I'd go bonkers. Back to work.

This time, I gave George the pirate book, and I picked up my school science textbook. The plan was for both of us to read one sentence at the same time, memorize them, and see if we could say them out loud. Go.

We stared down at our books. For some reason, I couldn't quite understand what the sentence I was reading was about. I looked across at George who was staring intently at the pirate book.

Then back at the science book. "Calories" — we'd done calories last week; it was easy. Why didn't I understand the sentence? Eventually I got it, and made George look up.

"A calorie is really nothing to do with how fat you are. It's a unit of energy."

George looked back at me, unimpressed. It was his go to say the sentence he'd read. He just stared at me. It hadn't worked. We swore in unison, then tried again, with different parts of the book.

"No part of this book may be reproduced without the publisher's permission," I told George.

"Seasick," said George uncertainly, after a pause. "Rough." I looked at the book, and remembered something in the story about a rough voyage. Then I realized that I had remembered it *while* I was reading about people not being allowed to copy the science book. I'd cracked it, but there was much work to do. I tried something else.

I lay on the bed, closed my eyes, and started my eleven times table. Easy till you get to eleven elevens. Meanwhile, George "looked" at the pirate book.

What a shock. It was as if I had unlearned to read. The pirate book might just as well have been in Japanese, hieroglyphics, or upper Martian. I stopped the eleven times table and the words came right, like a picture focusing itself.

I tried to concentrate on both at once.

Nine elevens are ninety . . . Captain nine . . . Johnson ten elevens are . . . snarled at one hundred and ten . . . the cabin . . . eleven elevens are? eleven elevens are? at the cabin boy . . . a hundred and twenty-one! . . . get me twelve elevens are . . . my sword and thirteen elevens are oh God, what are thirteen elevens? get me my sword thirteen thirteen thirteen and tell the crew what thirteen thirteens, no thirteen elevens scurvy dogs get me my sword and tell the crew . . . one hundred and forty-three . . . yes! tell the crew what scurvy dogs they are and that if any of them fourteen elevens . . . think fourteen elevens they can fourteen elevens . . . get round me, they'll walk one hundred and the plank, plonk plink oh hell, one hundred and fifty-four!!

Phew!! George and I looked at each other and laughed with relief.

"Get me my sword and tell the crew what scurvy dogs they be. Arr, Jim lad! And if any of 'em don't know their eleven times table up to twenty elevens, I'll keelhaul the lot of 'em, I swear!"

We were both laughing, when I looked at the clock. It had taken George half an hour to read one sentence, more or less without help. We stopped laughing. It would be a long job. I felt tired. We unsplit just as I heard a key in the front door.

4

As winter turned to spring, I began to make plans. First step – teach George more and more. Get him used to being on his own. We had a nice little routine going in the end. Most nights I'd get back home before Mum, make a sandwich (this always made me think of the juggler), take it up to my room, split, do reading practice till Mum came home. Unsplit. Do homework, get in a bit of juggling practice, with or without Lee and Terry, have tea, watch telly, go to bed. George's reading came on a treat, so did my juggling. I got much better than Lee, which made him a bit annoyed.

Soon the routine was come home, split, I'd do homework while George juggled, or vice versa. Amounts to the same thing, anyway. And by the time the Easter holidays arrived, we were *both* doing homework at the same time, one doing maths and science while the other did English or French. Tiring, but useful. I noticed that all this exercise made me (I mean me unsplit, by myself) read faster, catch on quicker, understand things more clearly.

I also sent George on little errands – to the shops, round to Lee's, or just out on a bike ride. I could always "tune in" to what he was doing by going to split screen, and always avoid the situation where we'd both be doing something really difficult at the same time. For example, if I juggled while he was out buying sweets, I'd have to stop while he went in and talked to the shopkeeper. Even that improved, though, and I realized that this was the time for a first major long distance, long term split. But there was something else I wanted to try on the first day of the Easter holidays. Something I'd saved up. Something I was really looking forward to.

"Gordon! Lee's on the phone! Where are you?"

In the shed, Mum, putting two tracksuits and six tennis balls in a bag. Then I'm off to the woods, where I'm going to start making showbiz history.

"Tell him I'm going out. Tell him I'll see him tomorrow. Tell him he's a wally!" I jumped on the bike, pedalled to the end of the road and let out an excited whoop.

I found "my" spot, the abandoned car. Deserted. I split. Changed into tracksuits. Got one of the tennis balls out of the bag. George walked

50

about fifteen paces away and stood, his back to me, looking away into the distance.

I threw the ball gently into the air and caught it, feeling its weight. George still stood with his back to me. Then without warning, I threw the ball as hard as I could at George's head. It would have passed his right ear, with about eight inches to spare. Would have. Except that George caught it firmly in his right hand. Then he turned round to face me, and we smiled.

George wore orange, because it was spelt a bit like his name. I wore blue. Both colours were bright, although one of the tracksuits, George's, was a bit old. I carried a schoolbag full of yellow tennis balls. About twenty in all. And a ton of cheese and pickle sandwiches, and a giant bottle of Coke, and a handful of emergency lump sugar. We carried identical very cheap pairs of mirror sunglasses, just in case.

Just in case anybody recognized us, I mean. A sort of half disguise. Me and George had never practised being twins in public. In the woods, unseen by anyone, we had practised juggling, throwing, talking, but no one had ever seen us. We couldn't practise being twins anywhere near home, though. Too risky. Imagine meeting Miss Greenleaf from school in Beckford:

"This is my twin brother I've been keeping secret for fourteen years."

"But Gordon, what school does he go to? Why isn't he at school with you? Why have you never mentioned that you've got an identical twin?"

Too risky. Even an hour's journey away, in London, there was always a terrifying risk, but the temptation was too great. So as we strode out of King's Cross station and looked for the tube to Covent Garden, we looked round warily. You never know.

This was the plan. As far as my mum was concerned, I was using up the first day of the summer holidays to start my science project, up at some museum somewhere.

Too good to be true? No. For a start, George's extra brain-programming ability had already made me a bit quicker at my work. My end of term report was really creepy. So much so that I'd got right up Lee and Terry's noses, I think. I started to realize that I didn't need friends so much any more. I started to feel confident for the first time in my life. And I was nearly six foot tall. Well, five foot ten.

So when I asked my mum whether I could go to London to see if I could find anything at the museums that would start me off on my science project, she smiled and said yes. Followed by a half hour lecture about the dangers of being kidnapped, murdered, run over, poisoned by cheapo food, sexually assaulted, pickpocketed, lost and being offered drugs.

So, there we were, on the crowded smelly indoor forecourt of King's Cross, having split in the 10p-in-the-slot lavatory. The staring was a bit hard to take, so we walked a bit faster. More staring. For God's sake, why?

Faster still, towards the tube. Then I realized. We were walking in exact step. We were synchronized, like square-bashing soldiers, with extra attention attracted by our rather loud clothes. A tiny effort, and we started to walk normally. George looked at his watch. My watch. Ten a.m. If our tests had been right, we had about six hours of split left. Maybe seven if we took it easy.

At the ticket office, I realized our other mistakes. Why not split nearer the square, and save money on tube fares? And why not take *two* bags, one inside the other, so George could share the load of balls?

As soon as we thought the words "load of balls", we started to laugh. In perfect unison. People on the tube platform stared again, and, with a tiny effort, we made our laughing different. This made us laugh more than ever.

I took out of the bag a really stupid-looking baseball cap. George put on his mirror shades. We looked at each other and fell about, and that's how we got on the train. A mad looking pair of identical twins, having a good time on the first day of their summer holidays.

We wandered aimlessly about the square for a while, looking at the expensive shops selling the latest fashions, books, records, wholemeal stripped pine muesli furniture, pictures and tourist junk. Then round the market, more junk. As yet, no one was busking. That's what I'd come to see. In particular, the hippy with the dungarees. Get a few ideas.

We sat down on some steps at the side of the market. The sun was beginning to get hot. Coke time. A swig, a time check, a quick thought about energy levels (A-OK) and a bit of a chat, for appearance sake only.

Then, a noise, getting gradually louder. Bedom DOINK, B'dom DOINK Bom b'DOINK . . .

We looked round. The noise was coming from a group of, well, youths I suppose you'd call them. One was carrying an enormous ghetto blaster, blaring out some jazzy funky stuff. There were about seven or eight of them, four black, three white, all trendily dressed in jeans, tracksuits like mine, trainers, one with a leather jacket, Walkmans, hats, loud T-shirts. They assembled in a loose circle, and rather sheepishly, they started to breakdance, bodypop, cartwheel and generally show off a bit.

A small crowd, me and George among them, started to form around them. It was hard to tell whether they were busking, or just doing it for the hell of it. They took turns to do their dance, some good, some not so good. Sometimes they stopped altogether, and then the crowd more or less melted away. Then they started again. Nobody, it seemed, was interested in collecting any money.

Eventually, we walked off round to the front of the market, where an even bigger crowd was gathering. In the middle, two foreign-looking blokes with guitars were playing. Pretty good. They looked like they knew what they were doing, much more than the breakdancing lot. After about ten minutes, they stopped and one wandered about the crowd with big canvas bags, asking for money.

"Spare something for the musicians?" he asked George. George stared for a moment, then gave the bloke 10p.

"What about your brother?"

"Sorry, mate, we're a bit skint," I said, trying to sound all streetwise.

That, of course, was what we wanted to become, and by hanging about the market, watching the acts and the tourists, we began to learn.

Round the side of the market was the "unofficial" pitch, often inhabited by the breakdancers. Some asked for money and some didn't. There was also a trick cyclist, "a real one, not a psychiatrist," I said to George, and we laughed, just for show. Then there was a really dreadful long-haired bloke with a guitar, and a loony who went on and on about God, nuclear weapons and the end of the world.

This lot didn't seem at all organized, and just started and finished when they felt like it, whereas the acts at the front of the market attracted a much bigger crowd, always took money, and seemed to have the whole thing sorted out between them. While one act – a magician who did a bit of fire-eating – was "on", another one was preparing behind him, under the arch of an old church.

At about midday, the biggest act came on, an all-woman band that played Sixties pop hits and rock and roll. They weren't bad. They were all about the same age as my mum, and for a moment we giggled at the prospect of her playing saxophone and dancing about to "Twist and Shout".

Despite their age, they were all dressed in sort of studenty-type clothes – jeans and baggy shirts with badges and stuff, and they all looked as if they had never seen the inside of an establishment called Monsieur René of Beckford, where my mum went every fortnight and came back complaining about the prices.

"It's double the price for twins," said the girl who was collecting money as the band went into some old rock and roll song.

We stopped thinking about Beckford. This girl was dressed just like the women in the band, but with more colour. She was our age, we guessed, and she was dead, well, dead pretty.

"Wow!" she smiled, fingering a bit of her blonde hair as she stared backwards and forwards, first at me and then at George: "What's the difference?"

"I'm the stupid one," said George. It was the first thing that had come into my head. I'd never have said anything like that if I'd been on my own. Girls, well, you know.

"I'm not so sure," she said, smiling at us and walking on without thanking me for the 20p I'd dropped into her bag. She had pushed a cheaply printed leaflet into George's hand.

LADIES EXCUSE ME – ROCK AND ROLL BAND, WEEKDAY LUNCHTIMES, THE KING GEORGE, FLORAL STREET. THURSDAY NIGHTS, THE LAMB AND FLAG, JAMES STREET. ADMISSION FREE. BE THERE.

By about four in the afternoon, we had the whole place sussed. Two possible splitting and unsplitting places, one a public lavatory round the corner from the square, the other a rather posher loo in a department store about ten minutes away.

Escape routes (just in case we saw anyone we knew), the different things that the "bottlers" (the people who collected the money) said to the watchers and the sort of act that drew the crowd.

Music was OK, but didn't get a big crowd for long enough.

Circus type stuff was better, as long as the acts were good. We saw a bloke on stilts trying to tell jokes who hardly got a crowd at all and a man and woman doing a sort of comedy magic act who got loads.

Round the side, the breakdancers posed and pranced, sometimes daring to collect (not much) money and sometimes not. We realized that this would be the spot for our debut, and waited for a gap in the action.

Maybe it was just a little too much. We strode into the space left by some bored hiphoppers and started. Three balls each, perfect unison. Then we started juggling them between us. Then, from spares in our trackie pockets, added four more.

From the corners of our four busy eyes, we could see the crowd get bigger, and our space get larger. Someone took a picture. The balls started to go higher. With no need for a prearranged signal, we suddenly jumped and spun, ending up so that we were back to back, about six feet apart. Applause.

Applause! Ever heard it? Ever had it meant for you? George and I smile in unison as we start to get to the end. A couple of complicated-looking crossovers, a sudden bit of fast bouncing (which is dead easy and gives us a bit of time to play with) and, still back to back, a couple of high throws. Then the balls get lower, we get closer, juggling gets faster. The difficult bit – the ten balls, one by one, drop into the front of our tracksuit tops. It's a trick, really. The first two we catch and just quickly stuff down there, freeing one hand each to hold the jackets open. The rest just drop in.

We turn and face each other, pretend to walk forward a pace to shake hands. Of course, with all those balls down our jackets we look sort of lumpy pregnant, which adds to the fun. Anyway, we miss, pass each other by, look as if we're nearly falling on our faces, and turn to take a bow. I saw it in an old film on telly. Silence. Then, as it becomes obvious it's the end, more applause. The hiphoppers and breakdancers eye us sullenly.

We vanish into the crowd, picking up our gear. Only when the "act" is over and we've walked away do we remember that we have forgotten to bottle.

"Lost our bottle," jokes George. We laugh, feel tired, make for the bogs, wait for a quiet moment, dive in, unsplit, go back to King's Cross.

The next problem, of course, is that we had to have an alibi. A reason for spending the whole day out, away from home. Notice that I'm saying "we" now instead of "I". It's sort of deliberate. We'd talked to someone (that girl, another reason for wanting to get back in there) and that someone had taken us for granted. We were twins. 'Course we were.

There were two possibilities, alibi-wise. One was Terry, who had a job, market days, on a stall selling cheap radios, batteries, car stuff. This could also help with the problem of explaining how I, a humble fifteen-year-old (or rather two fifteen-year-olds), was making money, because the next time we wouldn't lose our bottle. But Terry would himself have to be given a reason why I needed the alibi, and naturally, it couldn't be the truth.

The other was a development of the project idea. "School project, Mum, it's ever so interesting, it's about splitting the atom . . ."

No, too obvious.

"It's about insects, and I'm going to have to go to the Natural History Museum, the Zoo, it's dead important." All kiddy enthusiasm, yes, that would do it, and if I said that I'd occasionally call in on Aunty Laurel at dinnertime, or on the way home (Aunty Laurel worked in a big insurance office in the West End) it would clinch it. Now for the Terry alibi. And for Terry, there was going to be an inkling of the truth.

"Terry, you know your summer job on the markets?"

"No chance. It's my job, I found it, there's no way I'm going to let you in on it." We were in the park, mooching. Terry kicked a twig, and looked a bit sulky.

It was a good job, too. I didn't blame him for guarding it so jealously. Three days a week, Terry and this bloke who his father knew went to a different market. Terry helped unload the van, take money, go for stuff, load the van, take down the stall. They did their best business in the summer, so it was quite good money.

"No, it's not that. I just wanted a bit of a hand, that's all."

Terry drew on his cigarette. Poor Terry, less mad and less flighty than Lee, had started to smoke, although naturally his dad didn't know. It went with the working image. Me, I was six foot and had an inflatable twin brother and a promising career in showbiz. I didn't need to smoke.

"What sort of a hand?"

I stammered, looked at my shoes, went red, partly genuine.

"Well, there's this girl . . ."

"Girl?" He tried to make it sound like an insult. If Lee had been there he'd have been doing a girl act and trying to kiss me, taking the mick. I could hear him. "Dracula's daughter! Fifty pence says she is!" I could tell that Terry was genuinely interested – maybe a bit too interested, but it worked. And there was a girl, maybe, sort of. I didn't want my mum to know, so I wanted him to supply the alibi. Once or twice a week I was working with him, if asked. His dad's mate, or whoever, was expanding, needed someone to help out every so often. We trudged back towards my house to try the alibi out on my mum. Terry offered me a fag, man to man.

"Thanks, but no thanks, Terry," I said.

Terry looked a bit miserable. Maybe he wanted a girl, too.

I used the science project first, knowing it would be easier to sell to my mum. She was still worried, but she said OK. Next day, I started a routine that I would do twice or three times a week until . . . well, until disaster struck about a thousand times in one day.

No split until I reached the lavatories in the square, thereby saving the tube fare. A stroll round in tracksuits, carelessly chucking a couple of day-glo tennis balls about, looking at the stalls, drawing a bit of attention but not too much. The baseball caps and the shades helped.

On the side pitch, a bloke was doing some trick with a bicycle, while some hiphoppers looked on without much interest.

"Hey, look!" shouted a black kid. "Those two dudes with the tennis balls. The spacemen!" He came up to us – mocking but friendly. "You two are, well, weird, aincha?" he said in cockney Californian. "How much did the tube from Mars cost ya? Doing the business today? The act?"

"Maybe," said George.

Maybe. Try and stop us. And this kid had sort of given us a name. The Spacemen. Why not? We hung around the side pitch, limbering up, showing off, and keeping a look out for that girl. The breakdancers started, the black kid leading them. Pretty good. We limbered and watched at the same time, kicking, knees bending, stretching while we watched these four try and break their necks to loud music.

Of course, it was a mistake. Our concentration broken by the antics of the breakdancers, we started moving in unison. People started to stare at us rather than the breakdancers. We were sort of breakdancing ourselves – limbering to the music.

"Oy!" shouted the black kid. "Wicked! Well, wicked! Can you do this?" He did a sort of back flip and spin, turning like a gyroscope on the small of his back.

"No chance," I shouted. "We're jugglers, not contortionists!"

The breakdancers slowly drifted, but they left their sound system running. Without saying anything, there was a sign that it was now our turn, and we repeated our first time act almost exactly, only this time to the b'doink DONK, b'doink DONK of the ghetto blaster. Maybe it was a sort of dancing. Splatterings of applause at all the right moments. We grinned at each other. This would be even better if we were being watched by that girl . . .

George looked round – nearly dropped a ball – as we got to the end of the act. That girl wasn't there. This time, for laughs, we caught the balls in our trousers, so we ended up looking disgustingly deformed. Applause.

This time we didn't waste a second. We belted into the crowd, waving our baseball caps at people and saying "thank you very much" in mock showbiz language, like a pair of comics walking backwards off stage. Finally, the crowd melted and we went behind a pillar of the old church for a count-up. £9.43! Mind you, there were a lot of tourists and it was dead crowded. And we were good.

We sat under the arches of the old church, and felt tired for the first time. A couple of the other turns came past, smiling.

"Hey, I've got to go somewhere else this afternoon," an American girl with a guitar on her back said to us, out of the blue. "You guys want to take my space at the front this afternoon?"

"Sure. Why not?" me and George said together. The front meant the bigger space in front of the old market hall. You could get a crowd of about a hundred watching, plus the people on the terraces of the cafés and pubs. The big time.

We agreed a time, and started in on our

sandwiches. "Blast," I said, opening the bag. "You forgot to bring the Coke!"

"Me?" yelled George. "I thought you were in charge of all that."

"You wally!"

"Brain death!"

"Skunk breath!"

"Crumb bum! I'm thirsty!"

"So, you'll have to die of thirstation or go and buy another bottle."

It was a good idea, starting a row between us. Made us more natural. People looked at us and grinned. We grinned back.

"I'm sorry about my brother!" announced George, taking his hat off dramatically. "But he's just taken part in the world's first brain transplant operation – as the donor." The American girl, that black kid, who had drifted up out of nowhere, a couple of blokes with a magic act and some other hangers-about laughed. The little jazz band that was on at the front looked round for a moment to see where the fun was coming from, and the trumpet player made a braying noise that sounded like a laugh but fitted in with the tune they were playing. The audience laughed. We laughed. The other acts laughed. We were accepted. Someone shoved a full bottle of Coke under George's nose. He looked up and so did I. It was that girl.

5

"It's *impossible*," she said, peering at us. We'd moved into one of the outdoor tables of the closed pub in the square, and she was bombarding us with questions. "How do you tell each other apart?"

"We don't have to," I said, quick as a flash. "We know who we are."

Lisa (that girl's name) rolled up her eyes and tutted, but you could see she thought it was funny. "No, really! How does your mum know who's who?"

"She doesn't, sometimes," said George truthfully.

"But there must be some sort of difference!"

"Yes. I wear the orange and he wears the blue. Or is it the other way round?"

Rolled eyes again. She had a funny face, pretty, but a bit weird, somehow. Very long hair and very pale skin and very trendy but relaxed, not quite scruffy clothes, like lots of the people who hung round the square. She was sixteen, she said. Older than me. Us. No, wait. Together we're thirty.

"Who's the tallest?"

"He is!" we both said, pointing.

"The fattest?"

"He is!"

"The cleverest?"

"Me!" we said.

"The handsomest?"

"Me!"

"Who's the boss?"

"Him!"

Lisa laughed. We laughed.

"Here, do you want to hear my mum and the band? She's on in a moment. At the front."

Sure enough, we could hear the squeaking of saxophones and the tuning up of a guitar.

"We're on at the front today. First time," said George. "We must be on after her. That American girl with the guitar gave us her place." We all stood up, a threesome, suddenly.

I watched Ladies Excuse Me with some interest. Me, George and Lisa were at the side. Mustn't get confused with the audience. We were performers, not punters. I didn't understand why they were called Ladies Excuse Me and when I asked Lisa she was sort of humming and jigging along to "The Monster Mash" and didn't answer. No good asking George. I did, all the same, just for show. He didn't know. Surprise surprise.

There were six women in the Excuse Mes, as they were called by people who knew them. One on accordion, one on electric guitar, one on a big double bass, one with a lot of drums that looked like a pile of junk, one saxophone and one singing.

We studied them carefully, trying to work out which was Lisa's mum. I reckoned it was the fattish lady with the saxophone and George agreed. Frizzy hair that looked like it was just about to go grey but hadn't yet. The same slightly odd eyes as Lisa. Nice, but odd.

It was strange seeing women of that age – the same as my mum – enjoying themselves, all smiling at each other and jigging. Lisa's mum, in mauve boiler suit, mad jewellery and baseball boots, seemed to be the leader, and when she wasn't saxophoning she'd do this little steppy dance, swinging her saxophone, and the singer, who was really tiny so it looked dead funny, fell into the step and bashed a tambourine. They sounded good, and me and George found ourselves doing the steppy dance too. Out of the corner of our eyes, I saw Lisa seeing us, and all of a sudden we were dancing, the three of us, in a line. All doing exactly the same thing, as if we were going to break out into backing vocals or something.

"Your tennis balls!" shouted Lisa.

"What?"

"Do a bit of juggling!"

We didn't need it repeated. George fished in the sports bag and we started, first doing our act, then just making things up. George slipped round the back of the band and started lobbing ball after ball and I lobbed them back, the music rocking away as we got faster and faster, me turning round and round on the spot, throwing balls over my shoulder, catching them in my trousers, juggling by myself, then both of us dancing and juggling round the players who were all smiling and whooping.

"One more!" shouted the tiny singer, and somehow me and George knew it was nearly the end of the song and went to either side of the band, all the balls going like mad. The drummer hit the cymbals again and again as we caught the last balls – in our jackets, our trousers, our hats. George grabbed a tambourine and caught the very last one in that, with a satisfying crash.

The punters went mad, taking pictures and clapping and shouting "more!" Me and George just stood there grinning, then heard Lisa's mum shout, "Bottle! Bottle, for Christ's sake!"

We rushed into the crowd, waving our caps but still with shades on for security. Lisa was in there already with a big canvas sack, raking it in. Everyone was giving pound coins and fifty pence pieces as the band played on.

Lisa's mum *was* the one with the saxophone, it turned out. She was also the leader of the Excuse Mes. The four of us sat in a café round the corner from the square, tucking into a celebratory plate of fried everything. Well, me and George had the fried everything, but Lisa and her mum, Susan, were vegetarians, so they had it all but the sausage and bacon.

Susan was the exact opposite of my mum. She said shit a lot, smoked roll-ups, and Lisa called her Susan, not Mum.

"So who taught you?" she asked through a cloud of fag, which Lisa fanned away in exaggerated disgust.

"One of our mates taught us the juggling," said George.

"We just made the rest up," I added.

Both of them stared at us curiously as we finished the fry-up at exactly the same time. "Concentrate!" I said to ourselves. "We're different!"

I got up to look for the loo, leaving George to do the talking.

"It's incredible," said Susan, staring into George's face. "I count myself as pretty observant, but I'm buggered if I can tell the difference."

George winced at the word "buggered", and Lisa giggled. Her mother gave her a tiny look of disapproval.

"I can tell the difference," boasted Lisa, looking

at George, who blushed obligingly. "Something around the eyes."

"Have you ever been studied?" asked Susan, rolling another fag.

"How do you mean?"

"Well, there are some doctors who make a lifetime's work out of studying twins. You two seem a prime example."

George stared at his plate. The last thing we wanted was someone studying us. There had been enough of that.

"Maybe they don't want to be studied," said Lisa. "Maybe they just want to be rich and famous. I mean, have you ever seen juggling like that before? Bloody hell, we've had loads of jugglers here twice their age who weren't a patch on them. It must have taken you years of practice."

"Yes, years," I said returning to the table, glad that the subject had changed from anything to do with doctors and us being guinea pigs.

"Anyway, it's the same for anything. It must have taken you a long time to learn to play the saxophone like that."

"God, don't flatter her," Lisa moaned. "She'll tell you the story of her life. How she started off as a classical clarinetist. In an orchestra."

"Till you came along and I had to stop, and then I couldn't get started again."

Lisa obviously enjoyed this sort of stuff with

her mum. "You could have. Anyway, I didn't ask to be conceived. And if Dad hadn't gone off to America with his bit of stuff . . ."

Susan gave her daughter a look. The first Mum sort of look I'd seen her do. It said shut up or else.

"What does your dad do?" she asked, changing the subject.

"Sexist!" interrupted Lisa. "For all we know he stays at home and makes the tea and changes all George and Gordon's little brothers' and sisters' nappies. What does your *mum* do?"

I told her.

"And your dad?"

"Lisa, you hypocrite!"

"I only wanted to know."

Split second decision time. Should we resurrect Dad, the brilliant scientist? Should we make him something really boring? Send him to prison? Should we tell just a bit of the truth?

"Well, he was a sort of scientist, but . . ."

George couldn't finish, so I did. "He died when we were eight."

This time it was Susan and Lisa's turn to stare at their plates.

I decided to help them out of their embarrassment. "Talking about us being studied because we're so alike and that, my mum says that one of my dad's mates was going to send us to some hospital in Scotland because they wanted . . ."

I tailed off. Lisa and Susan were now staring at me, then George in turn. We had goofed. I could read their minds. They were thinking that I wasn't there for the bit of the conversation about us being laboratory animals. I was supposed to be in the loo, which they must have known was down a flight of stairs. I couldn't possibly have heard.

They were thinking I could read George's mind, and that probably George could read mine. They were right. Blast. It was one thing being jugglers. It was quite another having second bloody sight.

Lisa started to try and say something but it was obvious that she was having difficulty getting the right words. She was sort of pointing and gaping.

"Lisa!" warned Susan quietly.

The gape turned to a smile: "You can . . ."

"It happens sometimes," George explained. "Not all the time. Just when we've been . . ."

Time for a natural looking interruption, I thought. "Have you seen the time? Look, we'll miss our train." We both stood up and started grabbing our stuff.

"What about the share of the take?" asked Susan, rattling a bag of cash towards us.

"No, keep it. It was your set. Honestly. Doesn't matter," we said in convincing stereo.

"When are you back?" Lisa said to George, not me.

"Soon, the end of the week." We both turned to go, narrowly missing the waiter, laden with more plates of heart attack. He swerved and we swerved either side of him, but we swerved as one person. A couple of people looked up and smiled.

"Amazing," said Lisa.

On the train back, with George having conveniently disappeared in the loos round the corner from the square, I turned the day over in my head. First, the act. There were so many possibilities. And people really did like us. And the applause! And the money!

Problem number one. There was too much money. If we did three shows a day we could make tons more than in the imaginary job in the market with Terry. This was annoying because I knew Mum could do with it. So could we, for that matter. Maybe Lisa could look after it for us.

Problem number two. How not to attract so much attention, how not to have people going round saying things like "Oooh, they should put you under a microscope, it must be weird being twins, what's the difference, can your mum tell you apart?"

As for the cock-up about mind-reading, there was no answer except being extra careful. It was possible, if we were far away enough from each other, for communication to dim slightly, but if we got too far apart it could be dangerous, particularly with energy running low. In close range I couldn't help going split screen, me on one side, George on the other. As I was washing my hands in the loo, I couldn't *help* hearing the conversation. No, *having* the conversation. I was one person after all. Two bodies, that's all.

Problem three was that although I knew that I was one person, I was somehow developing a character for George, and a separate one for me. George was a bit quieter, maybe not so confident. I quite liked, as a private joke, for George to come out with the funny lines, but it made George appear to be the one with the sense of humour. It all came quite naturally. Or did it? I was quite tired as the train pulled into Beckford, and very confused. Lisa liked George better. And all right, I was a bit jealous.

But how could I be? George is me! How can you be jealous of yourself? Bong! An idea. I'd go back to the square next time alone. As George. Gordon could be ill, have a cold, or something. I got out the piece of paper to see when the Excuse Mes were on at the pub again.

One thing I'd forgotten to do that second time I went down to the square was to look in at Aunty Laurel's office on the way home, as promised. I just forgot, not surprisingly, really, when you think what else was happening.

"So how's Laurel?" my mum asked over breakfast the following day.

I decided not to lie. "Oh, I forgot."

"And Lee was round yesterday afternoon asking where you were. I told him you were either working with Terry or in London at the museum or just out. Honestly, Gordon, not even I know where you are nowadays. Why can't you spend more time at home? I hardly ever see you and you don't ever seem to see your friends any more."

Lee. Would Terry tell Lee that he was covering for me? What would he tell him? Lee was becoming one of those mates you wish wasn't a mate at all. And he could be dangerous.

". . . your own tea tonight because I'm going out. I said you'll have to . . ."

"Where are you going?"

My mum looked away. "Just out. With a friend."

"Who?"

"Someone from work. Someone I don't think you've met." She sounded slightly prickly.

"OK."

I helped her wash up, then went up to my room and split for half an hour.

George and I were learning more and more that summer. We could both read and write quite independently now at the same time. We'd got some insect books from the library and we

76

were quite genuinely getting on with the project, which we had to do for school by the first day back. Spiders, we'd decided on. Not really insects at all.

George would sit in a dressing gown (who wants to see their twin brother naked all over the place?) so we could unsplit in an emergency. We were also learning to use our strengths in a new way. More intelligently. Like you know when your teacher says list all the good points and list all the bad points and work it out from there? Or get into groups and decide who's going to do what, when? Well, me and George could do that quite well. Double brain power, almost.

For example, we'd always known about electrical things from really little. Maybe our dad taught us. I remember messing about with batteries. Anyway, one day my mum said she'd really like it if she could split the ceiling lights in the kitchen so we could have two instead of one. I persuaded her to let me (and George) do it, and one afternoon, while she was out, we got all the bits, then sat thinking out how we'd do it. Finally, we sorted it out. We didn't even have to use a ladder. I sat on George's shoulders, and he passed me up the bits and screwed bits together on the work surface, while above him I screwed bits into the ceiling, all at the same time. It took about a quarter of an hour, and it worked first time. You could see Mum was impressed.

Even when we weren't split I could make use of George's brain reasonably well. After a while Terry refused to play me at chess because he always lost, and he always used to beat me before.

Sometimes I took really big risks splitting. Like for a while I'd actually go to the shops while George kept reading, keeping really still so Mum wouldn't hear.

Once, she actually came up to my room while I was out. George had to leap under the bed. She just looked around, not touching anything, then walked out. God knows why. It worried me, though.

She was still a bit moany and prickly that evening when she got home from work. I'd no idea why. So I'd forgotten to go and see boring Aunty Laurel. I hadn't started World War Three.

At about six o'clock there was a hoot outside and she came rushing out, all done up like she was going to see the queen, gave me a big kiss, said sorry for being a nag and rushed out. There was a car, and though I tried to see who was in it, I couldn't.

Anyway, I bolted a huge tea, and by seven o'clock it was my turn to appear all done up. I had had a bath, washed my hair, cleaned my fingernails, blown my nose four times, dressed not in a trackie but sort of studenty casual, as trendy as I could, and finally split, leaving Gordon gawping at the telly, then going to bed early. He mustn't do anything strenuous – I was the one who was going to need energy. I was going to be George for the evening.

I had the piece of paper saying where the Excuse Mes were on that night (another pub near the square) and I calculated that the five hours I had between then and getting the last train home was more than enough time. I'd bike it down to the station, get the 7.07 and . . . "ding dong!"

Someone at the door. It was Lee. Shit.

"OOOooooh! Somebody looks smart! Going out, are you? Who with? Where you going? Can I come? Where's your mum? Out? Got any booze, has she? Going somewhere special? Can I come? Fifty pence says I can."

This was a joke from last year, something to do with our old English teacher. Lee was making for the front room and the telly as usual, while George, er Gordon, was climbing out of the window pretty sharp. Lucky it was summer, and we didn't live in a high rise like Lee. George or Gordon (take your pick at this stage) just climbed out as we walked in, Lee chucking himself on the sofa, noticing nothing and grabbing the TV remote.

"So, you're working with Terry, are ya? Lucky sod. Know what he told me? That I could have had the job and the only reason he never gave it to me was that I looked too young and his uncle or whatever was scared of getting arrested and put in the nick for slave labour."

Good old Terry.

I went out to get some drinks. "Won't be a minute."

During that minute, George (no, *not* George, GORDON for Christ's sake, George was going out) came down from where he was hiding in the spare bedroom and got two cans of Coke and I quietly slipped out of the back door, got my bike out and started pedalling like mad.

"Oh, I see you've taken your Sunday best off," Lee said to Gordon, as he went back into the living room and I crossed the High Street, hoping I'd not missed the train. I knew that Lee would make Gordon use some energy up, and just hoped it wouldn't be too much.

They stared at the telly for a bit. Then Lee started off on this endless story about taking his cat down to the vet to have it "done" because it had had too many kittens and his dad said he'd drown them.

"What's the matter?" Lee said, looking at Gordon. "Too gory story making you feel faint?"

"No, nothing to do with that. Only I was going down the doctor's," Gordon said to Lee matter of factly. "I wasn't feeling that well today. Sort of puky."

"You do look a bit odd, come to think of it,"

said Lee after a minute's gawping at the box. He suddenly stared into Gordon's face. Meanwhile I rushed into the ticket office, chained up my bike and caught the train by the skin of my whatsits. I sat in an empty carriage, completely panicked as the train drew out. Separated from George, sorry, Gordon, for so long with Lee there making who knows what sort of demands on energy, who knows what could happen?

We must have both looked pale with fright. Anyway, just as Gordon's signal from home started to go a bit faint because of the distance, I saw Lee stare at Gordon again and say: "You sure you're all right? You really don't look yourself. Fifty pence says you don't."

Gordon mumbled something about feeling really tired and a bit sickish and Lee suddenly got up, a bit sheepish and said: "You don't mind if I don't stick around then? You don't want to give me your lurgy, do you?"

After Lee left, it was all I could do to get Gordon into the bedroom and into bed, where he fell fast asleep on the spot. Mum would come back, stick her head round the door and think it was me all safely tucked up. Which, in a sense, it was.

In the meantime, he'd dream, of course. Of me and Lisa. Ten minutes to King's Cross.

6

I found the pub all right, and, judging from the noise, the Excuse Mes had just started their set. A real assortment of people: Right-on-yas from the offices round Covent Garden, arty types like Lisa's mum, Susan, people out for the evening having a drink before the pictures – and no Lisa.

I recognized the black cockney Californian, though. He was sitting by himself at a nearly empty table with a "'Course I'm old enough to be in a pub" sort of look and a drink that could have been a treble vodka and tonic or a glass of 7 Up. He caught my eye, pretended for a second that he hadn't, then, with a big act, shouted across the smoky pub: "Hey, freaky! Hey, Spaceman! Spaceman! Where's your wicked brother, man? Where the sci-fi threads?" For a moment it drowned out the Excuse Mes version of "Love Me Do" and everyone turned round, then carried on yacking, drinking, smoking, eating.

"How're they hanging, man?" he asked as I sat down. "Where's your bro, bro? You here to do your thing? Good God a'mighty, your stuff is wicked! All them flying balls! Hey, sorry. Zip."

He flailed his arm about and said it again, looking at me and smiling. I didn't know what he was going on about.

"Zip!"

I looked down at my trouser flies. Surely they weren't.

He nearly fell off his chair laughing.

"Man, it's my name – it's not an observation on the state of your chinos!"

I tried to laugh it off, not look embarrassed. It was weird – Zip reminded me a bit of a black version of Lee. Both little and noisy, only Zip spoke like something out of *Hill Street Blues*, but looked like a nearly streetwise, still a bit cutesy kid from *Grange Hill*.

"I'd buy you a drink but I'm skint," he continued, suddenly dropping the US for the UK. "Bloody Hiphop. I'd make more bread from a paper round. Lisa's always got cash. She'll be back in a mo' ."

She must have seen me first, because she was already walking up to the table (where she must have been sitting with Zip), smiling.

"Hi," she said, looking at me carefully. "Where's George, Gordon?"

I hoped she didn't see my face fall.

"How can you tell the difference, for God's sake?" Zip asked, pretending to stare deeply into my eyes.

I could have tried to bluff it out by saying I'm George but I decided to tell the truth. A bit of it, anyway. No point in starting a silly argument. Lisa had decided that she could tell the difference, so I was Gordon for the evening.

"George is at home with the flu. Generally whatever he gets, I get, but this time I'm staying out of his way."

Another flood of questions from Lisa: Did we share the same bedroom, were we in the same class at school, what school was it, where was it, why was I dressed so "straight", did we dress alike all the time, did we play tricks on the teachers, could we really read each other's minds?

Gradually the questions turned into a conversation, an ordinary conversation between two kids who sort of liked each other. Zip eventually Zipped off.

We discussed parents a bit – what it was like having a mum but no dad. Lisa had actually visited her dad in America by herself last summer. She and her mum and some of the Excuse Mes lived in a house near Kentish Town. She went to a trendy comprehensive where almost everyone except her and her friends was either the son or daughter of a famous person or terribly poor and deprived. She had just done her exams and was

going to do A levels next year then be an artist –
a stage designer or something. I wasn't sure what
a stage designer was.

I finally managed to tell her the story I'd
made up about us – it was almost true. Our
mum didn't know about the act and would go
up the wall if she found out. The hats and the
shades were a deliberate disguise, rather than a
stage costume.

"But how are you going to handle it? I mean
'cos you're going to be famous if you want to,
there's no two ways about it. There's never been
an act like yours, everyone's saying so. It's not
just you being twins, it's the whole bit – the
movement, the way you are with music . . .
my mum says . . . No, never mind what my
mum says, it's what I say. You want to develop
the comedy angle a bit. You're the straight one,
and George is funny. No, he really is! And what
about this mind-reading business?"

I looked down. I didn't want to talk about it.

"Let's get out of here," she said, standing up.
I finished the Coke she'd bought me, and looked
at my watch. Eight thirty. Last train from King's
Cross, 11.45. Energy level five. OK, let's get
out of here.

Lisa waved to her mum who didn't see her.
She was still engrossed in some song that was a
hit before somebody's mother was born, blowing
into her saxophone with her eyes closed while

little Suzy, the singer, belted out the song.

We wandered round the square where a few straggly acts waited under the street lights. The American girl folk singer, a magician, the trick bike man, but not many punters.

"So do you want to go for it or don't you?" Lisa asked as we ambled up one of the side streets towards Trafalgar Square. "You can't be a mum's boy all the time." That got to me.

"Look . . ."

She wasn't looking. She'd jumped into the road and was hailing a taxi, then bundled me into it.

"I've got to get back!" She ignored me, giving the driver directions. I felt a right twit. I could count the times I'd been in a taxi without my mother on the fingers of one elbow. Was Lisa rich as well as pretty? I felt out of my depth.

"Don't worry, Cinderella. I'll get you back for the last train to Hicksville before you turn into a pumpkin. I've got all the cash from that last gig and some bottle money plus my month's allowance from poor, guilty Daddy-o. We'll go back to Excuse Me Towers, have a nice cup of tea, talk things over and decide on a plan. Then I'll pop you into another cab to speed you back to King's Cross or wherever, and your ugly sister won't ever know. Nor will your pretty brother.

"Don't look at me as an over-confident sixth former, look at me as a manager. Can't you see it? A mind-reading pair of juggling identical twins backed by the best middle-aged feminist oldie band in the business! How can we fail? You can't sing as well, can you?"

I shook my head and looked out of the window, watching the unfamiliar streets speed by. Suddenly, maybe because I could feel the energy dragging a bit, I felt bewildered, depressed even.

Excuse Me Towers turned out to be a huge old house somewhere quite close to King's Cross. You could hear the trains going past. Lisa said that her mum had bought it when she'd split up with her dad, and then just invited women that she liked to rent rooms there, while she tried to get on with her career as a concert clarinetist.

But Lisa was only about two, and it was really difficult to find someone to look after her, partly because she was quite naughty.

"In the end, Mum started taking me to rehearsals, thinking that the music would soothe me. It was a bit of a last resort," Lisa said, stirring three sugars into my coffee in the huge kitchen.

There was hardly a bare bit of wall. Round the sit-down-and-eat-bit there were photographs all over the walls, some of Susan as a young, less trendy-looking type, of Lisa as a toddler, one or two of a man that must have been the dad in America.

"Anyway, I screamed and screamed during the loud bits. Apparently, the only music I liked was punk. Something to do with the safety pin."

"Eh?"

"In the nappy! I hope I'm not boring you," she added sarcastically.

"Oh no, I'm just a bit, tired, you know."

She didn't know, of course. I was trying to take it all in, make something of these people, who I liked, but who were weird. I stared at the other end of the kitchen, the cooking bit. There the walls were covered in pots and pans, sausages and garlic, colanders, those Chinese things, and other bits of kitchen stuff I couldn't put a name to.

There was a knock at the door and Jean came in with a tall skinny man I didn't recognize in artily paint-splattered jeans. Jean was the EMs' accordion player, who also gave piano lessons during the day and made cakes which she tried to sell to local shops. Later I found out she had a son nearly as old as me – a typical Towers dweller, Jean.

She and Skinny came into the kitchen, chatted a bit to me and Lisa about how the gig had gone while they made some sandwiches, then disappeared upstairs with them. It was always like that at the Towers, people in and out all the time.

"Love's young dream," said Lisa about Jean. "She's only been seeing him a week." We caught each other's eye, both of us embarrassed for a second.

As Lisa talked and talked, I tried to imagine her as one of the girls at my school, but couldn't. She was posh all right, but not horsey "my brother goes to public school" posh, like Fiona Redditch in 5A.

And she was probably a bit political as well (Anti-South Africa posters in between adverts for the London Symphony Orchestra). But she probably knew what she was talking about, not like Tara Smith who came to school every day with a different badge on, and pretended she was going on demos but always had a cold on the day and couldn't go.

"So finally the house got fuller and fuller of unemployed and semi-employed women musicians, and one Christmas they had a sort of jam session and everyone realized they liked bopping better than Beethoven and that's how Ladies Excuse Me was born.

"Look, enough autobiography. What I really wanted to say was I think you're both really going places, and sooner or later we'll get your mum sorted out . . ."

"But . . ."

"No, look, let's get this straight. I reckon what you need is someone who'll mould your act a bit, you know, say what works and what doesn't. A second opinion. Whether you want to work with the Excuse Mes or not. A bit of rehearsal, right? Maybe Zip can help. He's not got much to do any more."

Zip, apparently had been very heavily into graffiti art, and had gone out at night with the "crews", painting big sci-fi slogans that no one could understand underneath the motorways and once or twice on the tube. Lisa said he was really good, but he and a load of the others who were hiphopping in the square had been caught last month by the police, and although they didn't get sent to court, they'd got a caution and Zip's dad had gone spare.

I had half an hour before the last train, and I was beginning to sag even more. I looked at my watch.

"I'll ring for a cab. Here."

A fiver.

"Go on, take it, you earned it, and if we're all going to be partners . . . You will think about it?"

She rang for a taxi, and we went out to wait for it. It was a warm night, though the air smelt of London: meat, fags, dust, cars. "Ring me when you're ready to rehearse, and you come down here or I'll come up to Beckford."

"It's all right; best if we come down here. Have you got a garden?"

"Yes, it's a bit scruffy, but we can flatten it out a bit. Get Zip to help. Come on, here's your cab."

The taxi was crawling up the road, the driver trying to see the house numbers. I looked at my watch.

"Don't worry," Lisa said. "You'll make it. You do look tired, though. Maybe you've got the flu, too." She held the door open. "Just one more thing," she said, looking straight at me. "I was going to say this when we got back. Don't try that tricksy twin business with me any more. All right, to begin with in the pub I made a mistake, but it's the last time, George, OK? You are George, I know now. What's the point of pretending to be Gordon? So he's a bit stronger than you are but you're . . ."

She took hold of my hand, squeezed it a bit: "Even Susan says so, not that she's any judge of men."

Men? MEN?

Back in bed in Beckford, Gordon turned over in his sleep, and dreamed some more, as I took my first solo cab ride: "King's Cross, as fast as you can," said Lisa, shoving me in.

As soon as the cab pulled away, I grabbed the chocolate bar I'd kept in my pocket for emergencies and wolfed it down. I was starving. Next, I checked Gordon carefully. He was in a deep sleep, dreaming some rubbish about castles in a foreign country. The chocolate perked me up.

"What time's your train?" asked the driver.

"Eleven thirty-eight."

"No problem, as long as it's late," he chuckled to himself.

I checked my watch. We had six minutes. I had no idea where I was. The panic woke me up a bit more. Would I be able to run across the forecourt? Would I peg out halfway across?

Suddenly, we were there. I thrust the fiver into his hand, not waiting for change, and dashed through the doors. Hardly anyone about. I ran automatically towards the usual platform, then stopped to check the train boards. Wrong platform. Wrong way.

I heard the whistle as I got to the gate, rushed past the ticket man and alongside the moving train. It's not as easy as it is on the telly, getting a door open then jumping in as the train gathers speed. On the first attempt I slipped and nearly fell. On the second, I just chucked myself through the door, lurching across the carriage. A few faces looked up as I reached to close the door. Some smiles at my making it, a couple of people whose faces said what a yob. Pulling myself together, I walked down the carriage. Didn't want to stay with that lot. The other end looked emptier. I found a seat, sank into it, telling myself as strictly as I could not to fall asleep. I was pretty sure I had enough energy to stay awake and push the bike home at the other end. Just a bit tired, that's all. Luckily, a voice I recognized snapped me out of it.

"And I couldn't *imagine* commuting to London every day on these trains, it must be so . . ."

I looked up. Diagonally opposite me sat my mother, rabbiting on to a man I didn't know. Both held theatre programmes. She hadn't seen me, but I knew it would be only seconds before she did.

There was a moment's awkward silence. It lasted about a year.

"Gordon, what on earth . . . You didn't say anything about . . ."

I don't know who was more embarrassed. What am I talking about, yes I do. My mum. Here she was going out with a man for the first time since, well, ever, as far as I knew, because she didn't go out very often and when she did I almost always knew where she was going and usually it was Aunty Laurel's or a friend at work or some ghastly relative or my granny in Northampton who was in a home.

Not only was she embarrassed at me finding out she was going out with a man, she was also embarrassed – and probably very angry – that I was out on the town, the same as her, and she didn't know anything about it. The thing that made her more tongue-tied was the fact that she couldn't give me a good telling off in front of Whatsisname.

And Whatsisname was now looking on, smiling, which I suppose was a good sign. He was what you call an ordinary type. Balding slightly, suit, tie, glasses, nose, legs, teeth, you know the sort of thing. He could only have been an estate agent, or a bank manager, or a deputy headmaster – the one that does the timetable, not the one that shouts at people and hits them round the head.

"I've heard a lot of good things about you, Gordon. In fact, your mother's talked about virtually nothing else. Very nice to meet you, even if it is a bit unexpected." He held out his hand to shake.

"Gordon, this is Mike, who works in the South Beckford office."

"And your mum tells me you're very interested in the natural sciences, and that . . ."

"Bang!" What the . . .? I had to go split screen suddenly.

A block from our house, a car backfired loudly. There followed the usual round of dog barking. George woke up, bewildered. It was all getting too much for us.

For a couple of seconds, I must have gone completely off the rails. Mike and Mum must have watched me change instantly from the nearly sixteen Gordon – caught absent without leave and living it down like a man – to George, awoken from his baby sleep. On the train I closed my eyes, then opened them again, looking round droopily and doing just-woken-up actions with my mouth.

I managed to stay split screen and get George back to sleep without nodding off myself. Then I got back to the train in time to hear Mike say something about me probably having been drinking, in a matey matey sort of way. Mum smiled thinly. I knew I was for it in the morning.

And so I was. I talked it over with George, once we'd unsplit safely. We came to the conclusion that the best thing would be to take it all, say absolutely nothing to defend Gordon. Whatsisname had a car at the station, thank God, because my knees bent a bit when we got off the train.

In the car, my mum was entirely silent – the sort of dangerous silence that comes before a big row. I did snigger silently when, as we pulled up outside the house she said, "I won't invite you in for coffee, Whatsisname, I want to make sure that Gordon gets quickly to bed. We'll have a lot to talk about in the morning." Only she didn't call him Whatsisname.

7

Over breakfast there was silence, followed by a big telling-off plus interrogation. The excuse was that Terry and me had met some other kids and we'd decided to go to London and they'd got a different train because they lived the other side of Beckford. Yes, I had been drinking. No, I wasn't drunk just tired. No, I hadn't been taking drugs. Yes, I knew what drugs were. No, I don't know anyone who used them. Yes, I realize it was a selfish thing to do. Yes, I realize I was telling lies. Yes, I did have the whole thing planned.

"All going exactly to plan," said George from inside.

"So you planned to deceive me all along and just go to London without so much as a . . ."

"By your leave," said George silently. I held in a laugh.

"Gordon," said Mum in a suddenly I want to ask you a serious question although I'm still dead angry voice: "Were there any girls along on your pub crawl?"

I blushed convincingly. "What if there were? It's perfectly normal, you know – friendship with the opposite sex. Isn't it?"

She'd played right into my hands, just as George and I had discussed it, half asleep last night. Let her get out of steam being angry with me, then remind her she hadn't told me the whole truth about Whatsisname. *Then* rush off not giving her a chance to explain Whatsisname.

"I've got to go, Mum. Promised to meet Lee. See you later. Look, I'm sorry about last night. I'll try and be more considerate next time. I didn't mean to embarrass you in front of your friend."

She sat there, more embarrassed than I was. I was putting my breakfast stuff in the sink like Miss Goody Two-Shoes. Mr Goody Four-Shoes.

"Gordon, I'd like to talk to you about . . ."

"No time! I'm late! No, honest, Mum, I'm pleased for you – that you've got a . . . friend." Inside, George was falling about with laughter. "We worry too much about each other. It'll be fine!"

Funnily enough, it was. Fine, I mean. The interrogations got less heavy, she didn't keep asking where I was going (just what time I was going to be back) and I felt more like a free man. Men. Boys. Twins!

Me and George were still doing two performances on the days we went to London – one with the Excuse Mes, one on our own. We were even doing a bit of work on spiders – deciding that for our project we'd do a complete catalogue of the ones that lived in the South of England, and investigating the ones (when they came, which they did every year) that lived with me and Mum at Beckford.

Everything began to run more smoothly. The audiences were great, the money came rolling in and we became a sort of foursome. Us two plus Lisa plus Zip, usually. I could see Lisa was a bit more interested in George than me, but I reasoned in the end that you can't be jealous of yourself.

I did think of being George for a bit – wearing the orange trackie on the inside and swapping it so that George was the command module and I was the No 2. In the end we reasoned that it wouldn't work. George would become a bit more like me, that's all. And there was no getting away from it, I was inventing a separate character for George. He was quieter, somehow, not so confident. He came up with more ideas. He made the jokes.

"I reckon that you're the brains of this outfit and George is the true creative artist," Lisa announced once, as we hung about the square.

True to her word, she'd started "directing" us.

She told us how she'd "put a lot of work" into the Excuse Mes. She'd chosen a lot of the music, helped with their "image", even sorted out a few personal problems.

"They're all worse than schoolgirls," she laughed. "Two have been married at least once, and they all have dreadful relationships with the most unsuitable types of men. The only one who's the least bit stable is Suzy. Her boyfriend's OK – the sort of older man I'd go for if I went for older men."

She looked closely at George as she was saying this. George made a ridiculous, meaningless face, like a squashed grapefruit. She giggled.

On the work front, though, Lisa was anything but giggly. She made loads of good suggestions, with a bit of help from Zip.

The first time we went to Zip's house, because it had a bigger garden. I didn't know what to expect from Zip's family. We just went round to his house from the square one day, on the tube. Hyde Park Corner, then a walk.

I thought it was a joke at first. Lisa giggled at George and me as we stood open-mouthed at the gate of this drive. In front of us was this huge house, like a small Buckingham Palace almost, with a big lawn and a black guy doing gardening.

Me and George concluded immediately that Zip's dad was some sort of live-in servant. Luckily, we didn't say anything. I'd have been ashamed. Just shows you – never leap to conclusions. The man doing the gardening was Zip's dad.

He greeted us warmly, in an American accent. "Hi, Lisa. So these are the famous twins Zip has been so enthusiastic about. Well, if you're half as good as he says you are it's an honour for us to have you practise here on US territory."

As we walked onto the rear lawn Lisa explained that Zip's dad was a big shot in the American Embassy and that the house went with the job. Also that his dad had married an Englishwoman, accounting for Zip's odd double accent. And he liked gardening.

Zip had gone into the house and was now emerging, carrying his ghetto blaster. Behind him, an older black guy had a big tray with Cokes and a plate of overstuffed sandwiches. We ate, then set to work.

First thing, we chose a new track for the act. Zip had a huge collection of the sort of music that you can hear just as well outside people's Walkmen as in. A lot of shouting, rapping, bits of music, bits of people saying things very fast with bits of old record and scratching but above all the bedom DOINK bedom DOINK bedom DOINK all the way through. I quite liked it. Better than the Excuse Mes' golden oldies, although they were far easier to juggle to.

We learnt, mainly through Lisa and Zip yelling

at us, to juggle in time to the beat. First we all did some silly dancing – which looked less silly on Lisa and Zip. Zip was really acrobatic. Then juggling.

They kept on saying LISTEN TO THE BEAT, LISTEN! and jigging about, but they didn't realize how hard it was to get a rhythm and keep it. There was one particularly fast one which took ages to get into, and half the time our balls were on the floor (it's pretty easy not to laugh at that by the way, just think tennis), but after about an hour we managed it.

It must have been pretty spectacular too, because before long there was a little crowd out on the lawn, enjoying the act in the sunshine and saying "Wow" in American voices.

Then, while we broke for more Coke, George and I had an idea. Lisa and George were sifting through tapes and she said: "Chuck over the blaster," and for a joke, I did.

It was quite a big expensive-looking job, and although George had his back to me we knew we could go split screen and he'd be able to catch it without turning round. Just stick his hands out and catch it, like a football. We were only about four feet apart.

Zip saw and went absolutely wild with rage, his accents crashing back and forth from London Comprehensive to LA laid back (or rather unlaid back) as he went on about it being brand new and

101

having a CD and being "fuckin' PRECIOUS, man, know what I mean, so don' mess, right!?"

"Could you do that every time?" Lisa asked quietly, when Zip's fit was over. I read her mind. Or rather George read her mind and I read George's. Luckily, we had our own rehearsal GB, rather more battered and less valuable than Zip's. I grabbed it out of the bag, threw it over my shoulder and George caught it. He threw it back, and I caught it without looking. Then we put on a bit of a show, positioning ourselves facing each other, and tossing the machine back and forth, weighing it up, looking each other in the eye.

Then George yelled One Two Three and while the GB was in midair we both jumped round so we had our backs to each other. I automatically put my hands up in the air to catch it. Easy. Too easy.

When I threw it back, good old George fumbled and nearly dropped it. There was a gasp. The fumble was deliberate – we still needed practice at our most important lesson as performers. People had to believe that we might fail. Of course we wouldn't. For us it was as easy as one person throwing the machine up in the air and catching it. Not that easy because it was heavy. But we had to make it look a lot harder than it was.

The next throw after the fumble, George had a better idea. In one deft movement he caught the GB, turned it on full volume and threw it back.

Bedom Doink. We started to move to the music. A ripple of applause. The American audience had grown. Mustn't look round, though.

Then another idea. I hurled it high into the air, making it spin. The spin had a weird effect on the tape, making it go sort of wawawawawaw instead of Bedom Doink. More difficult to catch, too. More applause when George managed it. Not too many of those. Very tiring. When we did one the next time, we spun as the music went wawawawaw. More applause.

The logical next step – two GBs at once, facing each other. No way was Zip going to let us use his, but luckily, Lisa's trendy bag was lying on the ground, about the same size as a GB but probably less heavy. Without stopping the GB routine, I lunged and grabbed it, putting it in circulation with the GB. Cheers and more applause. We'd keep going till the end of the track, we decided. It was further away than we thought. The sun was hot. The concentration was sort of hypnotizing. I remembered the fish on the telly and the first split. I didn't know the track, hoped it would end soon. After about three months it did and we caught the bag and the blaster on the end beat. Neat.

We turned to our audience. At every window of the huge house and on all the balconies there were people, whooping, clapping, cheering. In the middle, like in some film about the first black man to be made president, I caught Zip's dad's eye. He was in a suit and now no one could mistake him for a gardener. We turned and bowed, like in the square. On the bow, alarm bells started to ring. I couldn't maintain split screen and we were getting dizzy. Too much heat. Instinct made us take two or three steps away from each other. Touching and unsplitting while we were unconscious would be a disaster. The big house spun like the ghetto blaster. Wawawwawa.

I dreamt we couldn't move. I slept. I heard someone say the word doctor and dreamt my panic. Fighting deeper sleep, I realized that energy levels were dangerously low. I forced my eyelids open. It looked like a very posh hotel room. Two doors. One open, a bathroom.

Lisa was sitting with George, who was on the other bed, staring at him silently. I couldn't go split screen. Zip was sitting with me and when my eyes opened, he yelled: "He's back, he's awake, he's conscious!" to be shut up by Lisa: "SHHHHHHHH!!!!!!"

Unsplit. That was the answer. Double the energy. Pretty damn quick. Not in front of Lisa and Zip, though.

Get them out.

Zip went out mumbling about where was the doctor.

I muttered that I was going to throw up. Lisa ran to the bathroom to look for something to come between me and the US property shag pile. Rushed out, no luck. "Vomiting's probably a good sign!" she trilled, trying to be bright. Rushed out of the door. I reached for poor old George – who looked dreadful – finding superhuman effort was needed to move an arm.

Unsplit! Hooray! I'm A-OK. I could feel the resumption of energy, like someone had turned on a light inside a dark room. I could hear some whispering outside, followed by Lisa shouting "gangway!" I jumped slightly dizzily to my feet, whipped off the extra trackie, chucked it into the bathroom and shut the door. She barged in with a bowl of fruit.

"It's a bit early for get well presents," I muttered, trying to look worse than I now felt.

Lisa ignored the joke. "Where's George?" she demanded, throwing the bowl's contents to the floor, and holding it under my chin.

I nodded to the bathroom. It didn't nod back. "I don't know what he's doing. Best leave him to it." If Lisa went and banged on the door and shouted, "George, are you OK?" I knew we'd be sunk. I hadn't got round to ventriloquism in the act yet.

She didn't. She sat on the bed with me which was nice and asked whether I wanted her to stick her fingers down my throat which wasn't so nice.

I made a brave recovery, smiling and explaining that it was probably just the sun and we'd be all right. I knew that given a half hour, a large dose of sugar and a small lump of luck I'd be able to recover, with enough energy for a short split. Maybe enough to get me to the loos at King's Cross.

Eventually, she got up to see where the doctor was. That was another problem. While I swigged at some flattish, lukewarm Pepsi that was luckily in the bag that had come up into the house with us, I imagined a kindly American doctor listening to our hearts or staring through a scope at our eyes and saying: "Hey! You're the most identical set of identical twins I've ever seen! I'd sure like to put you through some weird scientific-type tests to find out whether you're one person who can clone himself at will."

On impulse, I got up (boy, I felt better) and locked the door of the room. Then lay down again. Someone tried the door. Lisa, I thought.

"No more fruit for God's sake!" I called. "We haven't finished this lot yet!" I felt a right berk.

"Er, George, Gordon." The door rattled. It was Zip's dad.

I split quickly, checked energy levels, George leapt into the bathroom and dragged on his clothes, then lay on the bed and I opened the door.

With Zip and Lisa lurking behind him, in

he came, looking worried with his mouth but smiling slightly with his eyes. "I guess you two overdid it a little with the sun." Seeing him close up, you could almost feel he was important. He looked at us closely.

We took it in turns to say that sometimes the sun doesn't agree with us, maybe it was because of our fair skins, and we didn't need a doctor and the best thing would be for us to have a bit of a lie down and then go home.

Lisa and Zip both said we looked a bit better. We must have been. Split screen was now easy, although a tiny bit headachy.

"No need for a doctor? What do you think?"

"Don't think so."

"I tell you what I'll do. We'll leave you in peace for an hour or so, see how you feel. Just ring if you want something." I hadn't even noticed the telephone. "Then I'll put a car at your disposal to drive you home. Where is it? Hertfordshire, this young lady was saying . . ."

Something else we'd have to lie our way out of. Lisa'd have to help. Don't forget she thought our mother was the sort who would only let us watch half an hour's TV a week, and not let us out after 9.30 p.m. She'd understand that to return home in a chauffeur-driven limo might attract some unwanted attention. Ideally what we wanted was a lift to King's Cross.

Eventually they all left, and I locked the door

again and unsplit. I slept for two hours, undisturbed. I woke, finished the flatsi (flat Pepsi, puke) split and felt fine. Ready to face the world again.

8

I'd learned a lesson, though. I wish now I'd
learned it better. But that summer was so exciting, so busy, so happy, so mad — I suppose I
enjoyed the risks.

Oddly enough, looking back, I seemed to have
stopped asking why. Not much point, I suppose. I
felt that somehow if I did find out it would stop me
doing it. I stopped experimenting too. No more
crowds of naked Georges in sweet shops, no more
show-off "mind-reading". There was one more
experiment I was anxious to try, not so much
for our sake but for an audience's. Probably the
most dangerous thing we'd done. I was happy to
wait for the right opportunity. Not just a twenty
quid tourist crowd.

We did other shows, of course. Lisa and Zip
were always keen to find us different audiences
away from the square, just for experience.

We all went up in somebody's van to some

festival in a field. Vaguely political. No money. And the next weekend we all went to the opening of some Arts Centre in a new concrete town not twenty miles from Beckford. We were dead worried about being spotted, so we added a new bit of costume. Two bowler hats that Lisa had found in a junk shop and sprayed in our colours. They were a bit too big, and pulled over our heads they made our ears stick out.

Strange, the difference between that and the square in town. At the Arts Centre gig, there were no tourists eager to have a good time, so the audience was that much harder to get going. We managed, though, mainly by a tiny bit of extra clowning from George.

By that time we'd added another bit to the show. We got the idea when we were staying at EM Towers one night. A bit of a risk, but we were doing an early show in the square and I told Mum I was staying round Terry's because we were going somewhere the next day. We did it more than once actually, and she didn't seem to mind. Something to do with Whatsisname, no doubt.

Anyway, we were watching this old black and white comedy film, with one or two of the EMs and one of their boyfriends. One of the funnies in it was in his nightshirt going past a doorway and on the other side of the doorway his mate was playing a trick on him, pretending to be his reflection in a mirror.

Our version was a straight steal. The frame of the mirror was one of those clothes rails on wheels that some other act was using in the square. I walk past it in a big white nightshirt. George walks past it on the other side. I stop and stare in the mirror, poke my tongue out, jump up and down, and of course George does exactly the same.

I stop and look all puzzled. I turn so my back's facing the mirror. George doesn't turn. He knocks my hat off. I go for my hat, turn to the mirror and put it back on, and of course, when I look up George is putting his hat back on too. In the background the EMs are playing really stupid spooky-type music.

Eventually I walk through the mirror, and of course George does the same. Then I become the mischievous one with George trying to catch me out. Finally he walks away from the mirror and brings back – you've guessed it – a ghetto blaster. So do I. Then we jump out of the shirts and go straight into the ghetto blaster juggling routine. Brilliant. Mostly Lisa's idea.

Lisa, by the way, had taken to trying to get George off on his own. I'd got all this sussed by then. Neither George nor I gave her any encouragement, but we were both prepared, if necessary, to do a "let's not spoil our friendship" routine. The funny thing was that Zip appeared to be a bit jealous, and if Lisa asked George whether he fancied going to the café or for a walk, Zip would always go too. Poor old Zip. Poor old me to an extent, although I recognized, as it says in Mum's Mills & Boon books that It Would Never Work Out. All the same, when it was time for us to go, Lisa always kissed George goodbye in a different way to the way she kissed me goodbye.

One afternoon we were sitting around in the café. It was raining, the EMs had gone and me and George and Zip were counting the bottle money. This bloke came and sat at our table. Very scruffily dressed, but clean, if you see what I mean. Unshaven, slightly. He introduced himself, said how much he liked our act, and that we were bound to win the competition.

Some magazine was organizing a street act festival, with a competition to be held at the front of the square. The best act got a load of money and it was all going to be on TV. It wasn't for another three weeks yet, so I hadn't really decided whether we'd go in for it, because of the risk of recognition. I was being very restrained – not getting too excited in case I decided not to go in for it. Somehow, the George part of me was more in favour than the Gordon part.

Anyway, this journalist bloke, very well spoken and clever sounding, said he wanted to interview us for a magazine. Zip went all clever stupid and said he was our manager and that there would have to be a fee, and that he'd have to OK the photographs if there were any. The man laughed politely.

I wished Lisa had been there. She'd have known what to do. The bloke asked a few questions — how old were we, where did we come from and stuff. We were as vague as we could be. Finally he said, "Why don't you think about it?" and asked where he could get in touch with us. Zip thought it at the same time that I did.

"Why don't you leave us your number, and if we think it's cool we'll tinkle on your bell." The man laughed politely again, then wrote his name, which was James Morris, and a phone number on a café napkin. He didn't look like a journalist, but then I didn't know what journalists looked like.

Next day was Sunday. Usually that was a day I saw Terry (not Lee, who had begun to get on my nerves). I felt a bit sorry for old Terry. He'd decided to leave school and go full time with his uncle on the markets. He smoked all the time and talked about money a lot. I realized how much I was changing, and how much Terry was staying the same, in a strange sort of way.

Anyway, that Sunday Terry and I didn't meet, because it was Sunday dinner with Whatsisname.

I'd had a good idea about a caterpillar, which

could have spoilt Sunday lunch with Whatsis-name. Mike! I kept forgetting his name, and telling myself not to. After all, he was doing me a favour, of sorts. Without him to take her mind off it, Mum would have been on at me all the time, and I wouldn't be nearly so free.

I decided to let the George part of me do the talking at lunch. Much more charming and probably less big-headed. Good old George.

The weird thing was that the bloke seemed so at home. He was nice enough in a neutral sort of way, calling my mum Margaret and "love" at one stage. This wasn't a posh impress-a-stranger-type meal, it was a nice take-us-as-you-find-us sort, although the cooking – roast lamb, posh caky thing for afters, limited amounts of wine – was obviously designed to show what a good housekeeper and mother she was. Mother, moth, caterpillar, I thought. Shut up.

It's all right. I wasn't losing my marbles. It was a thought, spinning a web in my mind as George talked about spiders and how because we were a bit of a scientific family neither of us were really frightened of them.

"And they're supposed to be very good in the garden," offered Mike.

"But not quite strong enough to push a lawn mower," George joked, quick as a flash.

Mum looked slightly worried for an instant, in case Mike thought it was cheek, but Mike, seeing the joke, nearly choked on his broccoli. He was OK really, just so ordinary. The sort whose face you can't remember.

Mum laughed, relieved that it was all going so well. Later, after Mike had put on a big act about wanting to do the washing up, which was all right by me, because I'd said I'd do it, we went for a walk towards the sports centre. I met Lee on his bike and we stopped for a talk. Lee had seen Mum and Mike, and asked whether I was going to have a new dad. I said I didn't know, but if I was, it was a bit late. When I caught up with them they were holding hands. Somehow I didn't know whether to laugh or cry. So George laughed.

We were standing in the sports shop round the corner from the square, trying new lightweight trackies. We'd more or less decided that we'd enter the street act competition, and Lisa wanted us to cause a big sensation. She was right when she insisted that our old ones were too hot for the summer and not cool enough for style. So, out of the takings, we were buying two really cool new ones that just happened to fold very small. Dead handy for the unsplit journeys back and forth to Beckford.

We were trying them on when who should pass the window but James Morris, the journalist who wanted to interview us. He sidled in, smiling, and asked whether we'd decided. I'd talked it over with Zip and the answer we'd come up with was yes but no names and no photographs without shades or caps.

Lisa's reaction to Morris when we told her about him had been even more wary: "Look, supposing they do print an interview with you in the paper. And supposing your aunt or your form teacher or one of your mates finds out?" she said, a bit cross. She thought an interview at that stage would be very iffy – we had too much to lose. Her idea was to start attracting attention from the papers and the telly *after* we'd won a prize.

Me and George must have been mad not to think this through more clearly. It's one thing to be a semi-pro entertainer on the sly, it's quite another doing it full time in a blaze of publicity. And there was no way we could tell Mum. Instead of doing some serious thinking, we were more interested in prizes and new tracksuits and trying to look cool.

At least Lisa hadn't yet suggested that we all go to Beckford and tell Mum the truth, thank God. But she did mention that when we were eighteen we could do what we liked. Eighteen! We weren't even sixteen yet. Oddly enough, the competition was on the day before our sixteenth birthday. August 28th.

Anyway, it was just as well Lisa was in the sports shop. While we tried trackies, Lisa took

James Morris aside and asked him lots of earnest-sounding questions. We couldn't hear anything, but from the corner of George's eye we could see the bloke laughing in the nervous sort of way older people do when younger people ask difficult questions.

Finally, he marched out with, "OK, give me a ring if you decide yes," which sounded somehow insincere, even to me and George.

Lisa came back, we bought the trackies out of the Spaceman money and we retired to the arch in front of the square for a practice. Me and George hated practice. We were perfect enough as it was, we thought.

The day after was the one rainy day of that summer, and we were all gathered round the kitchen table at Excuse Me Towers for a meeting. The rain drummed down outside, and me and George tried to keep our minds on the matter in hand. Lisa was being irritatingly formal.

Present were Susan (representing the Excuse Mes), Zip, Lisa, me and George. Lisa, naturally, was in the chair. The agenda was heavy.

One: Would we like to go to see a circus next month at Battersea? Apparently, some bloke had seen our act and wanted us to see his circus. Not the usual one smelling of lion shit, but more modern, with rock and roll, comedians and stuff. He was, according to Lisa, interested in us, but no commitment either way at this stage. "Exciting, yeah? Your first real professional engagement! Should be good money, too."

Me and George were dead excited, but managed to keep a bit of cool. Zip made a joke about Nelly the Elephant.

Two: James wasn't a real journalist, as far as she could find out. Susan chipped in. She'd asked Jackie, the EMs' bass player, whose latest boyfriend was in the business. Boyfriend was a bit of a bad definition as he was in his mid-forties. Then we thought of Whatsisname. Then we thought of caterpillars.

"You two, are you listening or shall I go away and chew Nelson's Column for a while?" interrupted Lisa.

She was right. Recently our minds had begun to wander more, which was mad at this point, because here we were with what looked like a threat to blow the whole thing. We needed all the planning power we could pull together. If James wasn't a journalist, who the hell was he?

"Apparently, he doesn't work for the magazine he said he did and never has. What's more, no one in the news business has heard of him, and when I asked him, he didn't have his union card to show me and they all generally carry them all the time according to Jackie's bloke," Lisa said.

"But I don't see why anyone should want to — well, I suppose, *spy* on you, do you? I mean it's one thing for you to want to keep the thing quiet from your mum if she's a bit, well, toffee-nosed about the whole thing, but why have we got this snooper on our hands?"

Susan thought maybe it was a form of industrial espionage – somebody wanting to find out more about the act and how it worked.

We didn't catch much more of what she was saying, because at that point, me and George were silently discussing whether Lisa should be told the whole truth at any stage. Was she up to it? It would certainly help explain the caterpillar. But the caterpillar was too risky, I thought. It was clever, yes. But it could frighten people. George disagreed. Think of the looks on that audience's faces. They won't have seen anything like it . . .

"And three!" What a terrific finale to the act, even if we could never do it again.

"AND THREE . . ." Lisa yelled.

"Sorry, Lisa," George apologized meekly.

Lisa scowled, then couldn't hold back a soppy smile for George, just for a moment.

"OK. And three, we've all noticed that you two are getting to be a bit of a pain in the neck sometimes. We have to say it. Like just then.

"You've got all these people rooting for you. You've got your own personal band, non-stop help from me and Zip, and what do you do? You ignore what people say to you, you refuse to tackle your mum so we can plan your career, you leave your gear all over the place, you don't have a clue what the financial situation is. Like, did you know that you two have got about five hundred quid between you, after the Excuse Mes have taken their share? You're weird sometimes, you two. I mean money isn't the most important thing, but you don't seem to care at all."

It was getting through to us. We stared at the table, then looked up. Susan looked embarrassed. So did Zip. He was a bit of a softy at heart.

"It's for your good, man. You're too good to waste."

We looked round doing sorry-type faces at everyone. George, typically, was better at it than me.

Last on the agenda was the street act festival in the square, which was getting quite close.

"You're in if you want, with or without the Excuse Mes," Lisa announced. "The selectors saw you last week. I didn't tell you because I didn't want to make you nervous, or too big-headed. Anyway, Mum and the rest have decided that they'd be very happy to back you with live music, but they don't want to be considered as part of the act. You'll be separate in the judging."

It was a generous offer, and we said yes. Lisa knew that the big problem was the TV cameras.

"Look, you're going to have to come out sooner or later. And when you get your prize, who do they make the cheque out to?"

George looked at her, surprised: "You. You're our manager, aren't you?"

A few days later, I was idly drawing plans for the caterpillar at home when I should have been cataloguing house spiders, when Mum came in with a letter. We had another doctor's appointment. A check-up. This time, I hoped Mum wouldn't demand to come.

"If it's just routine, I'll tell you what they say. It's not as if I'm ill any more." I tried to be as convincing as I could, although something told me that the check-up could mean trouble, particularly if Mum demanded to come.

She said she wasn't sure. She'd think about it.

Lisa wasn't sure about the caterpillar. Not that we expected her to be. George explained it to her.

"Eight large hula hoops, right?"

"Right."

Pause to explain to Zip what a hula hoop was.

"Two bedsheets, thick, so that people can't see through."

I showed her the sketches I'd made.

"Then you sew the two sheets together so they're one long sheet, twelve foot by three, say. Then you sew the long edge together so you've got a sort of tube, twelve foot high."

Lisa and Zip looked blank.

"*Then* you sew in your hula hoops, so the

whole thing, once we're inside it, me on George's shoulders, looks like a huge caterpillar."

"Or me on Gordon's shoulders," added George.

"Then what?" asked Zip.

"Not quite sure," George said. "Loads of possibilities. Let's just make it and see."

I finally persuaded Mum to let me go for my check-up alone. I remembered the feelings I had about it the last time and told myself not to worry. Careless again. Kindly Dr Fowles just wanted to check again whether I was bonkers. Well, I wasn't. George might be, but I was totally sane.

I remembered quite clearly the last time I'd done the check-up routine with Mum. The big machine in the morning, then the posh house in Harley Street in the afternoon, the going over by kindly Dr Fowles and the mysterious man who didn't want to catch my eye.

It was a complete repeat. The medical, the machine, the trip to the Harley Street address. But this time there was no kindly Dr Fowles, it was Mr Weiss. Go straight in, Mr Weiss is waiting for you.

He was. I sat down opposite the big desk. Mr Weiss was a small thinnish man whose suit looked like an advert for suits, whose shirt looked like it belonged on an American TV programme about lawyers, and whose tie looked as if it had been tied, positioned and styled by a team of fashion designers. Glasses that were so rimless you could hardly see them but for a faint tint. I still had the faint feeling I'd seen him before. I think he was the man who bustled out of Dr Fowles's office last time round. Anyway, why was I seeing a Mr rather than a Dr?

"Gordon, I'm Edward Weiss, I've taken over your case from Dr Fowles who you may remember from all that time ago – what was it, eighteen months?" I was almost right. American.

I nodded.

"In case you're wondering, they call me Mr because I'm a neurosurgeon, not a psychiatric doctor, although I do also have expertise in that area."

Gulp. He can read my mind.

Gulp. He wants to remove George.

Gulp. He knows.

"Now, Gordon, at that time we discovered some real unusual brain patterns. I mean real unusual, unique even, and we decided that as long as you weren't suffering any ill effects from them, we'd wait before we did a full investigation until you'd grown up a little more. You follow?"

I nodded.

"So have there been any further side effects – weird feelings, depressions, headaches, double vision, bad dreams, anything at all?"

I shook my head. "Do you know what's causing the brain . . . ?"

"Hell no, but we'd sure like to."

"Are they dangerous?"

Mr Weiss looked down at nothing in particular on his desk, then looked up again. "Gordon, I've read your school reports. I've talked once or twice to your ma. And to your own family doctor. You're a bright person. I get the impression you see a lot but don't let on about what you see."

He paused for effect, staring at me.

"Now, as far as any medical danger is concerned, I'd have to hand in my doctoring badge if I was to tell you that there was no danger whatever. Probably not. Not right now. But the real answer is we just don't know. But I sure want to find out. That's why we'd like you to help us by coming into hospital here in London for a few days, maybe a week."

Mr Weiss smiled. He wanted, he said, to "hook me up to a computer in Los Angeles for a while, via satellite."

I laughed stupidly.

"Sure! I mean it! Medicine's gone a long way since you had that funky brain scan when you were fourteen. You'd be surprised at the speed things develop. And with a case as rare as yours, it's no expense spared!"

He wanted me to go home, tell Mum, pick up my pyjamas and come back that evening, but I said no way. An excuse about the spider project.

He was very interested. Or at least pretended to be.

Then he wanted me in the following Monday, but I was determined not to miss the competition, which was the Saturday after that. He agreed, finally, and escorted me across the huge office to the door.

"You know," he said, "your father – Harrison Watts, right? Great scientist. I met him once at a conference. Fantastic brain. Like father like son, I guess." He took my hand to shake it and looked me in the eye again. And I never guessed a thing.

We had a try-out with the caterpillar on the lawn at Mr Timson's (Zip's dad's) house, three days before the competition. As I expected, nobody liked it. Mr T. came down to watch, standing on the sidelines and looking faintly amused. Some other people, men in Mr Weiss-type suits, chambermaids, a gardener, and finally Zip's mum (who looked like a fashion model and was supposed to be related to three different foreign royal families in Europe) all stood on the lawn and watched me and George being told off by Lisa and Zip.

Of course we didn't do what we were going to do at the competition, just what we'd planned to lead up to it.

This was simply me getting in the caterpillar, then slowly juggling one-handed with George from inside it, while my other hand held the tube over my head. It looked like a man juggling with a giant caterpillar (a green sheet added to the effect), but it was a bit slow and not to the blaster beat. Then George sat on my shoulders and pulled the caterpillar tube up to his shoulders, and while I held the top above his head with two sticks, he juggled, so we looked like a ten-foot, juggling, green earthworm standing on all fours, if you see what I mean.

Then we just stopped, let the caterpillar down round our ankles, the hula hoops clanking together as they hit the ground, stepped over them and bowed. There was polite applause from the rehearsal audience, and sarcastic applause from Zip. Compared to the rest of our stuff it was rather slow, we couldn't help admitting.

"Drop it, you two. It doesn't work," Lisa said, trying not to sound bossy. "Just do the balls, the mirror and the ghetto blasters. My God, they're impressive enough. Come on, we've got an afternoon show to do."

On the way back to the square, Lisa started talking about us "coming out" and telling my mum that we were on the launching pad to some sort of fame.

"Look, if you're serious about this we've got to tell her some time. I've been very patient, but this circus thing could really be something. It tours all over, summer gigs only, so you'll be able to keep going to school if you want, and the money'll be good. But first you've *got* to tell your mum and you've *got* to do well in the competition."

She addressed all this to me. She didn't talk business much to George.

"I'll come with you, give you a bit of moral support. I don't understand you two, it's not as if you've done anything wrong. So you told a few white lies, so what? I bet once she's seen you doing the show she'll be as proud as anything. And suppose the circus thing comes off – you'll have to tell her then."

We tried to change the subject. We didn't want to do the afternoon show. It was a Thursday, and Saturday was the competition, then hospital. Lisa didn't know anything about that. I was getting sick of secrets.

I'd told my mum about what happened with Weiss, and she rang up our doctor who said there was nothing to worry about and this American, Weiss, was just after something else he could publish in his magazine that no one read.

Still, we didn't fancy the afternoon show. Didn't care about it. Suddenly the problems started to irritate all at once. Some of them, like the mysterious journalist who wasn't a journalist, Lisa knew about. Zip was now all in favour of ringing him up, tracking him down and finding out about him, but we didn't see the point. Best keep him at arm's length.

There was something scary about it, like something scary about Mr Weiss. And being scared makes you more scared. We hung about the square, where a TV company was starting to put up seats and ropes and cables as thick as your arm. They were already setting up for the competition. Zip, sick of long faces, decided to go and do some hiphop with his mates. Even the Excuse Mes sounded listless as they went on and did an extended set because finally Lisa could see we weren't up to it.

We three sat under the big arch and looked miserable. Lisa was worried that we were ill again. We shivered simultaneously (carelessly – we'd long ago grown out of doing everything except the act simultaneously) and fiddled with our gear.

Hard to say what we felt. First, that the summer was nearly over. Second that we couldn't put off realizing why we were like we were. Third, Lisa. Fourth, Weiss and the tests. Fifth, the magazine mystery. Sixth, although really first as well, the caterpillar. We knew that it would be going too far, but we still wanted to do it.

Lisa, it seemed, only read our minds about third and maybe fifth. She did this thing like she did when we were working together – being very fair with the amount of time she looked at each of us. Even when she looked sad she looked nice.

"So. What are we going to do then?" she asked, now not looking at either of us, embarrassed.

"What about?" Gordon asked.

"Well – everything." She paused for a moment. "Tell you what, let's wait until Saturday. After you've won. And don't *worry*." She aimed that at George.

9

Friday was the worst day of my life. It was worse than nerves. I hung around the house, trying to put all these photocopies of British spiders into some sort of order. Although I was alone, I definitely decided against any splitting. Conserve energy. Keep cool.

At lunchtime I thought I'd better go out, get my mind off things. The market was on in the next town to Beckford, so I grabbed my bike and rode out to see Terry. A mile or so into the countryside, my mind was beginning to clear. I was going through what I'd do tomorrow. Lisa had all the gear at EM Towers, including the trackies, the bags and the caterpillar. I'd get down there early in plain clothes, splitting at King's Cross, and we'd all go to the square in Susan's van. I went over the caterpillar trick in my mind, trying to work out a way of not making it seem too frightening.

I pulled the bike over to let a car pass, then realized the car, a big Volvo estate, was slowing down alongside me. Out of the passenger seat, someone was waving me down. I nearly lost my balance as the car pulled me in to the side of the road. The waver-down turned out to be James Morris.

I couldn't work out who was in the driver's seat. Morris got out of the car, smiling slightly. I stood behind my bike as he came towards me, wondering if I should fling it towards him and run. He just stared.

"Hi, George. Or is it Gordon? Sure you haven't changed your mind about our little interview?"

There was a definite moment when we sized each other up, as if a fight were on the cards. I said nothing. He knew I knew he was a fraud. He knew I didn't know who he was or what he wanted. Just when I was getting sick of the stupid staring-out, he grabbed my wrist. I tried to turn it away from him, putting myself neatly into a half-nelson. I shouted with pain.

The driver's door opened and a face popped up from behind the car. A black face. Timson.

"Leave him!" he commanded, like a man to a dog. Morris dropped my arm. I flexed it painfully, still saying nothing.

"Gordon, you'd better come with us," Timson said softly. "Mr Weiss wants to see you. Those tests he did last week. Something's gone wrong.

131

It's for your own good. Come on, we'll put your bike in the back, go back home to Beckford and take you on to Harley Street. Mr Weiss will talk to your mother, you don't want to scare her, do you? Come on, Gordon. It's all over now. It has to be."

We all stared at each other. Morris had that stupid grin. Timson tried to look trustworthy. I looked at each, then at my feet, then at the car, then at my bike. Then I buckled into pathetic tears against the car window.

I'd say about five per cent of the tears were real. Confusion and fear. Something to do with the depressed, careless feeling I'd had for days. Morris grinned even more, and Timson came round the car and put his arm round me. I let the bike drop in the gutter, and Morris had to step smartly back to avoid getting his shins scraped as it went down.

"OK, Gordon, get in. And hey, it's all for the best," he crooned, like an American soap character. "I've sent Zip out of town. He's got nothing to do with it. Just coincidence, that's all. Without him it would have taken a long time to track you down. Now, it appears that you're public enemy number one around here. I've had instructions. Washington, you know?"

"And Whitehall!" added Morris from the back.

Timson spoke quietly to me as he helped me

into the front passenger seat and shut the door. I don't think he wanted Morris to hear.

"Listen, Zip brought you to the house. Sheer coincidence. I mentioned you two to a friend doing research here, and he told someone else who knew about your father. That was coincidence number two. It's really nothing to do with me. They sent me to pick you up because they thought you'd trust me."

"I'm sorry about our friend here," he added very quietly, just before he shut the car door. "I have no control over him. The British insisted . . . take it easy now. You don't have to do anything. You're not going to be harmed."

Had he put me in the back I'd have been sunk.

But when I'd done my Oscar-winning boohooing act against the car I'd taken the opportunity to see that the keys were in the ignition. I'd also seen the magic letters P R N D L.

PLUNDER! Exactly. Automatically. While Morris and Timson tried to get the bike in the back, I slid quietly into the driver's seat. One chance, and a slim one at that. My first driving lesson, solo.

I twisted the key the wrong way to start, then looked up into the rear view. They were still having bike trouble. I twisted the other way.

The engine rumbled. I pulled the stick back like Biggles, stabbed the accelerator. The car roared and lurched. There was a clatter as the bike, not quite wedged in the rear compartment, flew out at Timson and Morris. The car was making an awful noise but not going very fast. I looked down and pushed the stick to D.

Tamed, the car slid forward and away. When I'd done fifty yards along the straight road I looked over my shoulder. What had started as a scene from a thriller had turned into comedy. Timson was holding the bike up and Morris was trying to get on and give chase. He was about as much of a cyclist as I was a driver. When I looked forward again I was on the wrong side of the road.

Until I hit the first corner, another three hundred yards on, the driving was easy. Luckily the road was nearly empty. On the first curve I swerved across the white line, then, swerving back, narrowly missed a signpost. On the second, I discovered the brake pedal.

I knew I couldn't keep this up for long. Once I hit even a small village I knew I'd also hit a little old lady or a vicar on a moped. I looked at the speedo. Fifty.

I passed a phone box, and realized that I had to talk to Lisa before it was too late. I swung the car into an old farm track, then behind a hedge, which I nearly demolished.

It was a risk calling Lisa, but I had to take it. Supposing they – who are they – had everyone's phone tapped? I ran back to the phone box. Ring ring. Ring ring. Ring ring. Susan.

"Susan, it's George. Tell Lisa to meet us this afternoon at Victoria Coach Station."

Susan iffed and butted. "When, George? Because she was going to do some shopping for me and we've got to get the van fixed . . ."

"Just DO IT! Look, sorry, it's important. And listen, don't tell anyone else but Lisa. We're in trouble." I put the phone down, went warily back to the car. This time I wanted to cry for real.

I sat in the driver's seat again and experimented. Moved the car gently forward, pretended I was steering round a non-existent corner. Finally I tried a three-point turn, got myself back on the road and headed carefully towards Ratchley. At first it was all OK, but as I got nearer Ratchley I started to lose my nerve. I practically died on a roundabout. On the outskirts of the town, I parked as neatly as I could, and trying to be nonchalant and seventeen, I locked the car. Then I carelessly dropped the keys down a drainhole and headed for the bus stop. I knew I had two hours' bus ride to think of a story. I was sick of lying.

At Cockfosters, the northernmost London underground station, I hopped off the bus. I realized that they, whoever they were, might be waiting for me to get off a bus at Victoria, so I'd arrive by tube. I got off at Leicester Square and dodged into a jeans shop. I examined my money. Just enough for a cheapo pair of jeans, T-shirt and crappy pair of trainers for Gordon. I'd decided to be George. I *was* George, dammit.

I couldn't find a lavatory to split in, so I risked going back to the shop and splitting in the changing room. No one seemed to notice. We had exactly enough money to get to Victoria.

Gordon went in the bus station first, while I hung about outside. Supposing we saw Zip. Was he part of it? And Timson? Why? The American connection with Weiss, obviously. And, the thought that had been nagging away for months, years maybe – something to do with my father. Finally, Gordon saw Lisa and yelled across to her. She scowled at him, and he ran for the exit so she had to follow him. Then, on the crowded forecourt, he changed direction again, looking round to check there was no one on his tail. Finally, I watched them come towards me on the split screen.

I was George and *he* was Gordon, wasn't I? But why? There was no time to think it through. Anyway, for some reason, panic, I suppose, it didn't seem to matter until I was face to face with Lisa, who looked very angry. Then it mattered very much. "George," she said to me. "What the hell's going on?"

We sat in a horrible crowded café near Victoria, me and Lisa on one side of the table, Gordon on the other. It was full of tourists and people with suitcases and children in pushchairs. Also at our table was a small man who was reading a paper and pulling at a thin, smelly roll-up. Lisa did exaggerated "I can't stand the smoke" signals.

We told Lisa what we had to, the half truth. Maybe we'd tell her the whole truth after the competition, if Timson and Morris hadn't caught up with us by then. It would mean our relationship, mine and Lisa's I mean, would probably end before it could begin properly. One of us wasn't a real person. We wondered whether Lisa would be strong enough for the full version.

We said that we were very weird indeed. Stranger than any other twins anyone had seen. Yes, we could read each other's mind. Yes, from quite a distance.

Lisa started going on about lots of twins being like that, of coincidences between twins who had been separated for years, yet married women of the same name on the same day, bought the same clothes, used the same toothpaste. We had, in the end, to show her.

Luckily, the little smoking man got up and left, and Lisa put her bag on his chair so no one could come and sit there. He'd left his paper, a *Sporting Life* – all horse-racing and numbers.

I asked her for a pen: "Now, watch."

I picked up the newspaper and opened it, then underlined one sentence. Gordon, sitting opposite, couldn't possibly have seen.

"King Samson's trainer, Mr T. G. Williams, said that the horse would be running in the 4.30, despite rumours of an injury . . ." he read flatly.

Lisa stared at Gordon, then at me, then at the paper, then at Gordon.

"Again," she said. This time she picked up the paper and underlined a sentence. I looked at it, and Gordon read it again, immediately, without looking.

Neither of us smiled. Lisa looked nervous. She opened her bag and brought out a book, a mouldy old paperback thriller. She opened a page, put it in front of me, cover straight up so Gordon couldn't see. She pointed to the first line. Gordon quietly started to read. She handed the book to him so I couldn't see it. I carried on reading. Then, we both read simultaneously. Then we took it in turns to say a word, one each. We could still read as fluently as if we were one person.

Lisa looked round nervously, as if we were in danger of being caught stealing the sauce bottle. We knew the questions she was going to ask. Gordon almost whispered: "We've been able to do it ever since we were little. Put a sweetie in his mouth, and if I want to, I taste it. Whisper in his ear, I hear it, if I want. It works . . . most of the time. Both ways. It's not a trick. It's the way we are. But when we juggle we're one person with four eyes, four arms, four legs."

"What about if you're a long way away from each other? The time you were with me and Gordon was at home?"

"Even then, usually. We don't like being a long way apart because it mixes things up," I said. "It can get very confusing. Uncomfortable. The point is that we're not freaks. We want to be taken for what we are, not poked at by scientists."

I explained about our (rather than Gordon's) check-up, and told her how keen the doctors were to do loads of tests on us, that we'd have to stay in a hospital, have all sorts of people study us, like animals. We thought of the trays of spiders in the Natural History Museum. All dead and labelled. *That* was what Weiss had in store for us, or something like it.

Lisa looked convinced. We said that until now we'd always refused to be tested, but now the doctors were saying that we were ill. We'd go mad if we didn't go into hospital. They called it help.

"And will you? Are you going mad? I mean what about your funny turn at Zip's? Hey, that reminds me, guess what, Zip's gone to the States, the bum. He phoned me up and said that he had to go to some family funeral in Washington with his dad, so he won't see you win the prize tomorrow . . . God, Gordon, you are *going* to do the show tomorrow, aren't you?"

"That's why we're here! Yesterday we had a

big row with our mum. She said that we had to do what the doctors said. She's scared in case we go crazy. Then she said that we'd have to be in for something like six months."

I felt guilty about these lies, but knew there was no alternative.

"We said no way because we wanted to do our exams. We're a year behind as it is, because we were ill. We didn't dare tell her about the competition, or the act, or anything. So we did a bunk."

Lisa said that our mum sounded awful, the first time she had criticized her openly, despite us moaning in the past about our curfew. This made me feel worse. Miserable. But I was determined to do the caterpillar trick. Show everyone, just once. And I was determined that somehow, I could make things OK between me and Lisa. So, after the show, she had to know everything. And if necessary, it would be Gordon, not George who would have to go. There was just one more excuse to make, and we hated making it.

We said to Lisa that we wouldn't stay at EM Towers tonight. We couldn't unsplit there very easily, and if Morris and Timson showed up there'd be trouble. I wondered again about Zip. His dad couldn't have gone to the States with him unless they both went today, after the bungled attempt to kidnap me. Who knows? We were beginning to get tired.

We explained to Lisa that we were going to stay at the YMCA, where some of the foreign acts were staying. We wanted to be all quiet and alone before our big day, but we needed some money because we'd come out in a rush. I could tell that she didn't believe us, and I wanted to make her feel better. So as we walked up Tottenham Court Road, I held her hand while Gordon, embarrassed, dawdled behind, pretending to look in the camera shops. She had her mum's autocash card, for some reason, so we went to get money. We did last minute plans about the act, and the gear we'd need, and we told her that I'd wait for the EM van outside the YMCA in Charing Cross Road tomorrow morning.

As soon as we left Lisa, (hoping that she wouldn't get a call from Morris that night but unable to do anything if she did) we dipped into an alley and unsplit. The YMCA turned out to be full.

I went back to the same cheapo store, which was just closing, and bought a sleeping bag. Then, round the corner, a toothbrush, and a ton of burgers and ten gallons of Coke. I found a phone box and called home. A risk, but I didn't want my mum reporting me lost to the police. I said that I was going to stay at Terry's that night. She put up a rather unconvincing fight. I thought I heard Mike's voice in the background.

Then I walked to Regent's Park and sat by

141

the lake, eating cold cheeseburgers and thinking about tomorrow. It was still warm as it got dark, and although the ground was hard and there was the occasional strange noise from the Zoo, I slept surprisingly well.

10

We sat in the back of the van and sweated. Through the window, we had an odd, porthole view of crowds going past, of clowns, tourists, policemen with dogs, technicians from the telly. We were itching to get out and join in the fun. We could hear the music from another act, two jazz guitar players who we'd met only once. One was American. Was he something to do with Weiss? Lisa agreed with us that it wasn't worth us mingling before the show. Not in our costumes, anyway. She didn't even want us to open the van doors, so we sat inside on the EMs' empty instrument cases.

The idea was to burst out and into the crowds when it was our turn, "make it more theatrical," Lisa said. The main thing for us was not to be nabbed. Lisa sat and waited with us, sewing these silver hatbands to our bowlers as a finishing touch.

No Zip of course. I didn't want to mention him, because despite what his father had said about Zip knowing nothing about the plot to kidnap me, I still didn't entirely believe it. I didn't want to think about him. Neither, apparently, did Lisa, because she didn't mention him.

We didn't say much, in fact. Apparently, there had been no visit to EM Towers by Timson, Morris or Weiss the night before. This worried us a bit, although of course we said nothing to Lisa. No visit might mean that they were watching the house, and knew we weren't there. Were they watching my house too? And Terry's?

We had stopped worrying about who they were or why we were "dangerous". We had stopped worrying about everything except the act. As long as we were just allowed to *do* it, caterpillar and all, that was the main thing.

Gordon had glued his face to the van's back window. I was counting tennis balls for the fifteenth time. Suddenly, a head came right up to Gordon's on the other side of the window. It had a policeman's cap on. There was a tap on the window.

"You know, this van's not supposed to be here. Can you move it as soon as you can, otherwise you'll be completely hemmed in."

Lisa flirted with him in an obvious way, which seemed to do the trick. She told him she was far too young to drive and we were part of the show and the driver would be coming back soon and then we'd go, and isn't it a nice day and she hoped he was enjoying himself, although she could see he had an important job to do.

During all this me and Gordon skulked at the other end of the van, fiddling with the caterpillar. We couldn't be too careful. We'd already had one stroke of luck that morning – that it was a different van because the Excuse Mes' usual one had broken down the day before. Timson and Morris wouldn't be on the lookout for this one.

"What's that for?" the copper asked pointing at the caterpillar, genuinely curious. The caterpillar hoops made it look, half folded, like a basket. "Got snakes in it?" He ambled off, grinning. Well at least that showed that the fuzz wasn't after me. Just the secret service of the whole Western world, so that was all right.

I knew that Lisa was against the caterpillar routine, although she didn't (couldn't) know what it was for. All the same, I felt I had to warn her, somehow.

"Look, there's something else about the caterpillar – something we've never done for an audience before. It's a trick, right? Just a trick. It'll fool everyone, but it's . . ."

There was a bang on the door. Susan. The signal. The EMs would go on, do two numbers, "Charlie Brown" and "Twist and Shout". We had to leap out of the van and leg it across the road into and through the crowd and be there at the end of that.

Last minute check. The coat rail was in place in the arena, in front of the EMs' gear. Just the caterpillar, the balls, the ghetto blasters. Batteries? Check. Balls? Check. Energy? Last swig of Coke. Check. Gloves? On. Very important, gloves.

Shake it up, baby, now. We felt sick for a moment. Lisa grabbed us and kissed us both. "Fame! – here's to it!" she yelled. Then she opened the back door of the van and threw us out, like parachutists jumping from 50,000 feet.

We leapt into the crowd, all of whom were jiggling to "Twist and Shout". Lisa followed as we battled through them. When people turned and saw us, trackies, bowlers, shades, gloves in colours as loud as the music, they stood aside, laughing and pointing.

We were at the edge of the arena bang on time, with the EMs doing a frenzied jump up and down bang-a-boom finish to their set. Loads of applause, whistles and yelps, half quietened by little Suzy's ringmaster style announcement.

"Ladies and gentlemen, the two and only . . . SPACEMEN!!!!!!"

The band launched into the juggling number and we jogged into the arena, put down our stuff as if this was a Thursday afternoon audience. Then we looked up. Click.

The photo is still printed on the back of my

brain. The size of the crowd, stretching right back as far as you could see. They'd built low terraces for people at the back, and there was a big platform right in the middle with TV cameras pointed at us. Another mobile camera right at the front of the crowd. The first floor balconies of the pub *behind* the arena were jam-packed too, and on both sides of the arena the crowds bulged against the barriers.

Behind us under the arch, on both sides of the EMs stood the other acts, policemen, TV people with clipboards and headphones, a couple of photographers.

Click. No time to scan them all for Weiss or Timson or Morris or Dr Fowles or Lee or Terry or my mum or anyone. I'd lost Lisa for a second, then, turning to get the tennis balls out, caught her eye. She was next to a TV person. We smiled, the three of us, and then belted into the act.

We'd never, ever been so good. We strained to look a bit "ragged", went berserk with the number of tennis balls, kept everything to the beat, dead on.

For the mirror routine we relaxed a bit, which meant that our movements really were as close as mirror images. The crowd roared with laughter, edging forward to get a better look.

We threw the ghetto blasters higher than we ever dared, sweated and swaggered, oblivious to

147

the applause and the whoops. At one point, the mobile cameraman at the front got between us and dangerously close to being killed by a falling hiphop briefcase. The audience bellowed and screamed as we stopped for a moment, wiped his brow, then ours, with the discarded nightshirts from the mirror routine. Then we started again.

The caterpillar. One spaceman inside the caterpillar. Other spaceman outside caterpillar. Spaceman juggles with caterpillar. The tension in the audience went, as we'd expected. This was tame stuff after the GBs. Spaceman One allows caterpillar to drop. He's now standing in what looks like a wastepaper basket. He beckons to Spaceman Two. Spaceman Two comes over and sits on Spaceman One's shoulders. The crowd are a tiny bit restless now. This doesn't quite measure up to the juggling or the comedy mime. Never mind, they're expectantly patient.

The caterpillar skin is pulled over Spaceman One. Spaceman Two sticks out of the top, juggling two balls. Slowly, the skin moves up over Spaceman Two's head, so that in the end, he disappears.

The EMs' drummer gives us a roll on the drums, but doesn't know when to stop. The crowd clap politely at the ten-foot juggling caterpillar.

Inside the caterpillar, Gordon (at the bottom) helps George off with his trainers. George takes one glove off and Gordon takes one glove off. In their mind, they consider saying goodbye to each other, but don't. They just think it. Then George reaches down and Gordon reaches up and they very nearly shake hands. They just touch.

The caterpillar collapses immediately, a waste paper basket again. Spaceman One stands alone, in an orange tracksuit that looks a bit lumpy. Everyone stares.

Then Spaceman One lifts the empty caterpillar over his head and holds it out to the audience, a hollow stubby tube. A peculiar near-silence. Only the people at the back who haven't got a clear view are talking, trying to find out what happened. Few people notice the spare pair of trainers on the floor, or the second bowler with the shades inside.

The people on the pub balcony behind the arena have had the best view. They are the quietest. One or two look sick.

Gordon, now wearing George's orange track-suit, turns all the way round, looking through the empty circle of hoops and cloth at the shocked faces. Few of them are smiling. Click. Another one for the album.

George's reappearance takes more time. Gordon lifts the tube, then, inside, takes off the outer track suit. Splits. It's crowded in there, and there's a danger of unsplitting again, so on go the gloves. George struggles back into his trackie and is putting his second trainer on when the tube comes down to reveal the return of the invisible spaceman.

Crash!!! A loud, slightly off-key fanfare from the EMs, with a drum smash at the end. The faces start to smile again, and there are cheers, gasps, relief. Everyone begins to feel it's OK again and the applause and shouts now thunder. No time to catch Lisa's eye again. Something tells us not to.

To one side, a crash barrier moves and two or three punters, wild with excitement, try and come into the arena to shake our hands. A policeman tries to stop one of them. They rush towards us, trying to take pictures, slapping us on the back. One, who looks drunk and has a stupid slogan T-shirt, gets tangled with the mobile TV camera cable. The other, coming towards me, wears a sun hat and very black shades. He has his hand out in an elaborate handshake gesture.

From behind, one or two of the acts are coming forward to congratulate us, or maybe protect us. He's only five yards away when I recognize black-shades as James Morris. He's only five feet away when Gordon sees the syringe tucked into the palm of his hand.

Other crash barriers are down now and there's no distinction between arena and audience, just chaos. We sink back into the little crowd that is swallowing us up from behind, getting as far away from Morris as possible. Lisa fights her way through, and makes a grab for Gordon, who is being swept away by a friendly ten-foot copper. She manages to grab hold of George, instead, and drags him backwards and off to the edge of the square.

Meanwhile, the friendly copper is yelling at the crowd and shielding Gordon at the same time. Both of us are feeling danger signs on the energy front. Too much sun, too much excitement. Gordon and George silently arrange to meet at King's Cross as soon as both can get away.

Lisa and George are now sitting on the edge of the pavement on the opposite side of the square to where Gordon is still struggling in a crowd which contains James Morris and the syringe. Another barrier goes down, catching Gordon in the chest. He sinks to the floor and is scooped up by the ten-foot copper. Half of George's split screen goes dead.

By the time I'd come round, waited for the St John's Ambulance lady, given a false address to the ten-foot copper, tried to stop falling asleep on a camp bed in the first-aid enclosure, waiting for a doctor who never came, drunk a cup of hot sweet tea, fought off the pain in my chest but not my head, George and Lisa were at King's Cross. We got the split screen going once or twice, but the pain was too much, worse than the time at Timson's.

I worked out that I was probably Gordon again if I wanted to be. I couldn't work out why I'd been George, or when we'd changed over, but I knew for certain that whoever I was I was in more danger in the first-aid enclosure than anywhere else. I could be grabbed at any minute. So I just walked out through the thinning crowd. The show was over.

First I tried to get back to the EMs' van, which had gone. There was no sign of Susan or any of the others. I was tired, didn't quite know what was going on. Everywhere I went, people stared, not getting too close.

I'd lost the shades and the bowler. I'd lost George.

I walked away from it all, dangerously exposed, and started towards King's Cross, my head and my heart pounding. I couldn't think straight, but I had to rest again.

I changed direction again, and made for the park, walking very slowly. Within seconds of getting into the park, I knew I had to sleep, and knew, at the same time, that if I did, I might not wake.

I must have looked innocent enough – a sunbather, a youth who'd had too much to drink and was now sleeping it off or a tracksuited jogger who'd overdone it. I dreamed that I was on the train back to Beckford, then realized, waking, that it was George who had been on the train. Why?

Did Lisa put him on it? Did he just get on out of habit? Was he escaping?

When I woke the park was nearly empty. I got up carefully, tried to go split screen. George was at Beckford station, alone, sitting on a bench, staring at a litter bin. Into his field of view came uniformed trousers, a bit of stretcher. I managed to wonder why he'd got on the train. Faint voices and a quiet siren, but the head pain was too much for me to stay with him.

I felt in my pocket. Luckily, there was one pound coin and one 50p in there. I needed sugar desperately. I dawdled to the edge of the park and into the street. For some reason I got on a bus, then got off without paying my fare. I walked painfully up a street I didn't recognize in a part of London I didn't know. It was getting cooler. The sky was darkening. Found a phone box. Rang home. No answer. Rang Lisa, although couldn't remember the number at first. Pushed in 50p when someone answered. The phone went dead.

Found a café. Ordered a Coke. Drank it. Went split screen for a split second, heard faint bleeping, smelt a hospital, heard quiet voices, saw nothing.

The man behind the counter in the greasy café is staring at me. I've been in here for an hour now, and only had one Coke. While I sit, George feels further and further away. And I feel more and more tired. Mustn't, mustn't, *mustn't* go to sleep. Should I ask the man for another Coke, then pretend I've lost my money? He doesn't look the understanding type. But I've got to get to George. I'm not even sure if I can stand up any more. And what if George dies? He can't. He mustn't.

11

Quite recently I asked Ed whether I could ever have children. We were sitting in the TV room and he was drinking his umpteenth cup of coffee.

He smiled. "You'll have to give me a while to think about that one," he said. "You haven't got any plans right now, have you?"

I'd thought about it a little for the past couple of days, but I couldn't work it out. Would they let me? Have I been "done" already, like Lee's cat? Would they be splitters? Would they let them be? I don't know.

The two years went slowly, like twenty. The first month I didn't speak at all. Hardly got up, even. I didn't know where I was and I didn't care much. The room was like one in a hospital, with a few extra comforts. At first I couldn't speak. I don't know, maybe they had me on drugs of some sort. I could hardly sit up I felt so knackered. Then I just didn't want to speak. Why should I? What was there to say? I watched TV a lot.

My mum came, tearful and white, but I couldn't even talk to her. She rabbited on about being sorry and why hadn't they told her more about Dad and she was so stupid and it was all her fault.

I was a complete bastard, because I never said it wasn't her fault. I still didn't want to know.

Ed Weiss spent a lot of time in my room, not saying much, watching me eat (which I did rarely) and asking me the odd question which I didn't answer.

All I knew was George was gone for good. Dead. Was he ever alive? Who cares, he wasn't any more. They'd taken him. Killed him, if you like. I knew that whatever they'd done to me in the first, unconscious days, it had stopped me splitting. I knew, without trying, that I'd never be able to do it again. I'm not sure how I felt about that. Sometimes I felt angry, I felt that they'd taken away something that didn't belong to them. Sometimes I felt relieved. No more worry about finding a place to split, awkward questions, being caught.

One day, Ed came in as usual and started talking. I could tell he was slightly angry, trying to control it, though.

"OK. You want to know the whole story?

Yeah? Come on, Gordon, you do, don't you? Or are you so stupid and stubborn you don't care any more? Or just a little bit scared? Not strong enough yet, huh? Huh?"

I stared at the TV, which had the sound down. I flicked it up with the remote. It was him that broke for a moment, not me. Grabbing the TV cable he ripped it from the wall, leaving the plug in place.

He sat down and lit a cigarette, sighing. I tried hard not to remember how Lisa used to react when someone lit up, and managed to croak "OK."

So, this is what he told me. First, where I was – on a barely used American air-force base in East Anglia, in an isolation suite used for pilots who'd cracked up, astronauts who'd seen little purple poodles and the odd visiting senator or vice-president who doesn't want people to know he's visiting, specially if he's using the suite for what the papers call a love nest. Ed's words, not mine. He looked at me carefully during the love nest bit.

Anyway, it's a cross between a hospital ward and a luxurious flat. A bedroom and a sitting room with a TV, computer, video and stuff. Reminds me a bit of Timson's house. Impersonal, somehow. There's also a little corridor, an office and a porch – a tiny bungalow in the middle of what to me looks very like nowhere.

In the porch stands Stanley or Craig or Rick. Big Americans in suits and macs. Security. In the office sits Ed and his nurse-secretary, June, also American. I sit in the bedroom or the lounge, amusing myself on the computer, reading, talking to Mum on the phone sometimes.

Why all the Americans? Ed Weiss told me the story about a week after I decided to speak. He also told me I had to believe it because it was the only story he was going to tell. He talks like this all the time. A logical smart arse, but I began to stop hating him, then I managed to like him a bit. It's all supposed to be for my own good. I'm not sure what my own good is any more, that's the trouble.

I never asked anything about my father, which surprised Ed. In the end, he told me, starting very cool and deliberate, and getting more and more excited.

Dad's where it started, of course. And Ed is the man in the photo, a much younger Ed, without the sharp suit.

Dad was doing research with an international team into plant reproduction. The idea, as Ed put it, was to "teach grains to do more of the growing work, rather than leaving it all to the human beings".

Here my understanding starts to get a little hazy. Ed, who is my tutor as well as my doctor and, I suppose, my guard, says that if I want to understand it I'll have to learn it all myself. He won't get in my way, won't hide anything, but he won't help either. He means that what I should do is get educated and become a scientist. I'm not sure I see the point. I've had rather a raw deal from science.

Ed told me that two years before I was born, Dad's team discovered that DNA had "an extra dimension" in all living things, and that my father was the first to see into that dimension. Harnessing what he saw to an enormous power source, he thought he could develop what he called a "genetic photocopier", except that all the materials for the copies – the ink, the paper, the chemicals – could be found in the original rather than in the stationery shop.

Ed's words again, not mine. Ed, who when he gets going is a bit on the big-headed side, has a cartload of degrees. "If we all used the letters we had after our name, we'd have to have all our mail in extra large envelopes," he joked once, showing off. He was the man brought in to provide the sort of electric power needed to "get into the hidden molecular programme", and it was American money and technology that got them, beavering away in Cambridge, to the state where, on paper at least, "we could make one corncob give birth to another, identical corncob. Like in the Bible!" All deadly secret of course, so the only people to know the whole story were those who needed to.

And the British and the Americans both had to play a part in it, and apparently they were always squabbling. When I was caught, it was a toss-up whether I was given to the British and nasty James Morris, who I never saw again after the competition, or the Yanks and Ed. No one thought to ask me. I'm only a guinea pig around here. Oink. The Yanks won in the end, on the condition that I stayed in England until they'd finished with me. According to Ed they have to hand over all the research on me to the British eventually.

Anyway, when he got to the bit about my father being able to split, he started going a little peculiar, the only time I'd seen Ed not quite in control. He said that my dad was "irresponsible" and was "risking the experiment by taking it further than the brief we had set ourselves."

Somehow it didn't come as a shock that my dad could split. Nor did it really shock me that the splitting killed him. What was hard to handle was that he killed himself deliberately, or seemed to.

"Harrison wasn't thirty-five when this started happening to him," Weiss said. "Hard to say whether it was an accident or not. Whether he was experimenting on himself. He certainly didn't understand it fully, in terms of what it would do to his mind. Not like you. When you came to it you were young, right? Flexible. It grew up with you.

You can't teach an old dog new tricks, I guess."

The square came back to me. Lisa, juggling, the caterpillar. Just tricks, I suppose.

"He also wasn't to know that it was hereditary – that he'd pass it on to you . . . the point was that he just got out of control with it. There was no science in it any more, just a crazy danger. He told me, demonstrated to me. That nearly drove *me* crazy. Imagine your friend and colleague showing up at your house half nuts with excitement in the middle of the night, then showing up again and sitting next to himself on the sofa.

"I ended up with *me* needing help, but there was no way I could go to the Embassy shrink and tell him. This was strictly need to know. Anyone not directly involved in the project couldn't be told anything. It would still have been secret but for his craziness. I'm sorry, Gordon, but that's the only way to put it. It made your father nuts, it put a lot of people at risk, and in the end our security wanted to know why he was never at work on the project and what the hold-up was.

"Your ma never knew, though. She hardly saw him. Oh, she knew something was wrong all right. She'd come to me and beg me to help, but the only way I could was to get Harrison to stop splitting which he would not do. No way. He'd split and stay home nights while the other Harrison worked on in the lab or went joyriding even.

"Most times I saw him I never knew whether he'd split or not. Sometimes he'd laugh or talk to himself, sometimes he'd threaten me, sometimes he'd try and convince me to experiment on myself."

This was obviously painful for Ed, and I could see he was treading carefully. He didn't want me to know too much.

"After he'd threatened me a bit I called in our scientific security people, who watched him. Only those who saw believed, until we had videotape. Even then some didn't.

"It ended up with no more than a dozen people in the world who knew. Me, Morris, the president of the United States, who scientific security worked to – I don't think the president understood it – your home secretary (who was an eyewitness one night when Harrison decided to demonstrate) and some security people. They decided among themselves that I was to be his minder, try and get him off it.

"There was no question of further experiment. It was all too dangerous, too spooky. Nobody liked the project, nobody trusted it any more. He and I were our own little scientific nuthouse in a semi-secure laboratory complex in . . ." Weiss stopped himself. He'd got a bit carried away.

"Finally, when you were born, or maybe just before, he stopped, or at least he said he did. It was real hard to tell after a while. When you were small, he was very wrapped up in you, but . . ."

I realized while Ed spoke that the dim memories I had of my dad may well have been memories of half a dad – while he was playing football in the park with me he could have been somewhere else at the same time.

"Well, it had to happen. After a while, he just couldn't resist. More self-experiment. By then we were both crazy, him more than me, and at the height of our craziness . . . one night, I found him in the lab, dead. His skull had been smashed in once, with a fire axe in the lab. He was wearing two sets of clothes."

Weiss looked at me, watched me as I grasped it. An important lesson.

"Well, Gordon, you're probably more able to judge than me, or anyone else alive. What do you think happened?"

I saw the scene in my head. An ugly fight, my dad's splitter (or my dad himself, or a combination of the two, a double decision, maybe) picking up the axe, hitting then unsplitting before death.

"Murder or suicide, Gordon? And what might the motive have been? Simple confusion, or something else? Jealousy perhaps. Who knows?"

So, here I sit, day after day. I jog round the near empty base with Craig when he's on, and occasionally we have to duck as some huge winged

163

bomber swoops over. They've just given me a little jeep to run around in, within the wire, and I can go to the PX and the cafeteria and sit with the senior officers, all of whom have been briefed that I'm security orange so no questions asked. They generally treat me like an idiot with leprosy.

No one worries about me escaping because they know how afraid I am of going out. For a year I never left the suite. After a long period when I hated Ed, then tolerated him but didn't trust him, I grew to like him and even depend on him. He was the only one I could talk to, him and his tape recorder and his notebook. I know I can't cope with the world till I've coped with all this. That's what Ed says and I agree, I guess.

Listen to me, I'm even beginning to talk like him.

That café – the one that I ended up in, where Ed found me, staring into space, energy almost gone. Although I don't quite know where that café is, I can see it in my mind's eye as clear as anything. If I could draw I'd be able to put all the detail in, right down to the colour of the man behind the bar's teacloth and the feeling I was going to sleep for a million years. At around the same time, Ed's men must have found George on the platform at Beckford in more or less the same condition. By then we'd lost all contact with each other.

Ed started me off there, every time we had a

session. It's how he got me to talk first, making me remind myself of the last bit of "real life" before I was caught. He'd always start those sessions with "OK, Gordon, the café, you're there alone, you don't know where George is and you know time's running out." Then he'd get me to describe something about it – my Coke bottle, the ashtray, the cheap travel posters on the wall, the menu.

It never failed to bring it all back.

Then he'd say something like, "OK, Gordon, from the café, take me back to the square when you started your act," and I'd be away. At first I was suspicious, thought it was some sort of hypnosis.

"Do you feel hypnotized?" Ed asked.

"Nope."

"Are you in control of your thoughts?"

"Yep."

Ed is a brilliant question asker. Should have been a TV interviewer or a detective.

The bit that most interested him about my story was the time I split more than once in the sweetshop. He was always asking me to go over stuff again and again, prodding me gently for more and more detail. How did I know I could do it? How did I feel? How did the woman react? How did I react to the other three Georges? Could I move them? Could they think? How many split screens did I see? Did I ever do it again?

"Maybe we should have run more tests," he said, more to himself than me. "We couldn't do too much while you were unconscious and we were stabilizing you, and everyone was too spooked when you woke up. No one wanted to risk it."

I asked what they would have learnt.

"Exactly," he said firmly. "We knew the project was over, had to be. What was there to gain?" Then he looked up at me as if he only just realized I was there. As if he'd been having a conversation with himself.

"Maybe you're not going to be a scientist after all . . ."

I didn't understand.

"Well, what you might call a true scientist will investigate a new thing not because he thinks it'll be of any benefit, but simply because it's new."

"Seems sensible to me."

"But sometimes it comes unstuck."

I get lessons from Ed, well, science and history at least. I watch TV, I sit at the computer, I do more work on spiders. During my silent period Weiss bought me a vivarium with seven different genera in and I, like a spoiled kid, chucked it on the floor, where it smashed. The spiders scuttled away to become US citizens.

Mum comes, with Mike, who's been vetted. She knows, but pretends not to because she can't cope with it all without being upset. Mike thinks I've got some rare disease from exposure to radiation, which in a sense is true. He brings me chocolates, like a baby, though I quite like him. I definitely approve of him and my mum, who seems to be a lot better recently. Ed and I drink beer occasionally.

Once, during one of our "bull sessions", after I'd told Ed my story, he asked me whether I thought splitting was morally wrong. A sin, sort of. It was a confusing question. He talked about it being "against nature". I thought of the warplanes flying overhead, secretly stuffed with atom bombs. I asked Ed whether he thought they were against nature too. He lit a fag, but didn't answer.

He wanted to talk about Lisa a lot, too.

"OK, supposing you had told Lisa the full story . . . demonstrated to her," he says in a lecturerish way, gesticulating with his pencil. "And suppose she was able to cope with it. And suppose you had a . . . full relationship. She'd have had to have you both. You might just as well have been joined at the hip, like Siamese twins.

"And when you unsplit, as you had to do after seven or eight hours, what does Lisa do then? Who are you when you're one person? Does Lisa like that one? Is he different from the two you are when you split? That makes three altogether. How do you handle it?"

This time I didn't know the answer. Maybe they were right to come and get me.

Three weeks ago, Timson came. The same kind black face, the same film star personality. I suppose he betrayed me. No, it was George he betrayed. Would George have killed me? Ed said try not to think about it, which was weird coming from him, a man who wants everything under the microscope.

You could tell that Timson was trying his hardest to do a "no hard feelings" routine, although I think he was quite sincere.

Both Ed and Timson hadn't a kind word to say about James Morris. He was by all accounts a real nasty type, and the reason he got heavy with me was that I wouldn't play the interview game. Morris's first idea was to interview me and George together, to get a picture of what we were like as two people. When his plan failed, he got really unpleasant, according to Timson.

We sat talking and reminiscing about the Spacemen rehearsing in the gardens of the big house in Mayfair, and I told them that the first time I met Timson I thought he was the gardener, which made them both fall about laughing. Later I begged Timson and Ed to let Zip come, but it was no dice. Anyway, he was in California, about to learn to become a film cameraman. No kidding. His father swung it for him. Timson is a powerful person.

"He was far too interested in you for his own good," he told me. "You've got to understand, you were a dangerous person to know. For someone like Zip, a diplomat's son with a tendency to be a little wild, it was all too risky."

I could just see Zip at film school. In his element, forgetting all about his cockney side and the graffiti business. I can see him, with a megaphone and a cast of hundreds, shouting, "Let's make movies!"

So Zip was nothing to do with it. Not guilty, Your Honour. They snaffled him away really fast, as soon as Timson and Morris had caught up with me. If he ever comes back maybe he'll contact Lisa. He definitely fancied her before I came on the scene. Maybe they'll just forget the whole thing.

In a few years, on a visit to the UK to promote his first feature film, Zip would say: "Hey, Lisa, remember those weirdo twins we used to know? What in the world happened to them?"

What would happen if I ever told anyone my story? Sometimes I really want to. Would anyone believe me?

OK, so what did happen to the weirdo twins? When, after about three months of regular visits back to the café, Ed and I had pieced the whole of my history together, he told me how George had been disposed of. I was angry for a bit. It had taken days telling Ed my story, from the first split to the last disastrous one. It had all gone down on tape, with Ed gently questioning me, asking me to go over something again and again, how I did things, how I felt, how I controlled energy, what I thought of George and him of me.

"They" hadn't known until the time at the Timsons'. It really was a coincidence. Timson happened to describe our act to a friend in the Embassy who was interested in genetics and had known about a small part of Dad's project. He brought it to Ed's attention. Before that, they'd monitored me but were sure I was normal, but for my brain patterns.

Ed had to tell the British, which was where James Morris came in, and I had to be brought in.

I'll never know how or why George went back to Beckford that day. Not unless I see Lisa again. Lisa is now nineteen or twenty, I'm eighteen. No chance, I reckon.

Anyway, in a sense, they killed George, sort of. The idea was to get me before I did the act, because they were worried that I'd do something "difficult" in public, which I did. The caterpillar was bad enough. Had I split into three or more in front of their very eyes, like in the sweet shop that time when I was a kid, it would have been a big problem.

As it was they had to fall back on starting a mini-riot, because they couldn't find me before the show. I was saved by the EMs having a different van from the usual heap.

In fact, it wasn't their only bungle. They lost George before he got to King's Cross, and they lost me completely, only finding me by luck in the café. After the caterpillar, they'd pulled out all the stops, with literally hundreds of people looking for us in London and Beckford. They watched our house, Lisa's, even Terry's and Lee's.

They put me in one helicopter and George, who'd been found unconscious on Beckford station, in another. We unsplit here on the base. Ed says he was the only one in the room. My poor old ma had all but collapsed with the strain.

We were unconscious for a bit, and everyone was saying "touch and go". Ed arranged therapy for my mum.

I asked Ed once what would have happened had we stayed apart, for longer, after the competition. He said that the material that was George would have started to "break up". Now no one would ever try it, because no one would be allowed to follow in my or my father's crazy footsteps. I asked about George "breaking up" and Ed paused for a moment, searching for a comparison.

"It would have been like your whole body having a sort of, well, cancer, that accelerated at maybe ten thousand times the rate a normal cancer would. Total collapse. Any medic who didn't know the whole story would have been completely freaked. If I'd got to George when that had started to happen I'd have had to terminate him real quick. Don't ask me what would have happened to Gordon. Instant brain death? The same break up? Who knows? We just got to you in time, that's all."

Once we'd shown we were going to recover, they designed a "Corrective ECT" for me. Electro Convulsive Therapy. Ed says he's ashamed about this. He says it's like smashing a beautiful and complicated piece of equipment with a sledgehammer. It blots out a good bit of brain, including the bit where George lived. Sometimes I wonder what else has gone.

Ed and I had long talks about why this had to happen, and after I heard about what it did to my father, I sort of agreed, although I was still very confused and quite tired all the time. Ed says I'll think it all through in the end but it will take a long time.

I still haven't explained how they killed George, not properly. Because Lisa, Susan, the Excuse Mes and various other people in the

172

square still believed in me and George as twins. We were flesh and blood. They had polaroid pictures. They knew us.

The TV was easily disposed of. When they played back the competition the next day, the tape of our act had been destroyed, somehow. "Technical problems". Dirty tricks by Ed's men: a break-in at the TV station. All clever secret service stuff. They didn't pinch the tape, they just wiped the Spacemen bits on it, and a few others so there'd be less suspicion.

There had also been a slight disturbance during the act. Some "yobbos" had started trouble. There was a little news item on the TV about that, Ed said. There were some injuries, none very serious, but neither the TV company nor the organizer wanted that sort of thing in the programme so they simply cut out what was left of our act. It was either unusable or wiped.

But according to the papers and to local TV and radio news:

A sixteen-year-old competitor in Saturday's street theatre festival in London died after a sudden heart attack yesterday.

George Smith, from St Albans, half of the juggling duo called The Spacemen, had suffered from a heart complaint since birth. It's thought that the attack was brought on after disturbances at the festival interrupted their act, and by Saturday's intense heat.

George's twin brother, Gordon, is said to be in deep shock.

Then a smudgy tiny photograph, which could have been anybody.

I imagined Lisa watching the news, or hearing it on the radio. I wondered for a minute what she'd do, whether she'd try and track Gordon down. Ed only showed me one article, but said there were more. I could watch a tape of the local news broadcast if I liked, but I didn't want to see any more. I felt tired.

So, what about the future? Wait and see, says Ed. He wants us to go to the States, all three of us, Mike, me and Mum. Mike and Mum are getting married next month, and the wedding will mean the first trip out for me, if I feel like it. It's a bit nerve-racking really.

When I'm well enough the plan is to do some exams and go to university. Ed keeps jokingly trying to tempt me about college life in the States. "Natural sciences, yeah?" he says, like natural sciences were a football team that deserved complete loyalty. I don't know. I read a lot, I like the papers, the magazines, the TV news, the serious talk.

I also want to get fit. Run more. The other day when no one was looking I tried to juggle with fruit I bought from the PX. It reminded me of the hippy who started me off on the idea.

I'm rusty, but it's still there, the old juggling. It's all in the wrists.

Maybe I'm less scared of the world than I was before. Maybe I should be less influenced by Ed, with his rimless glasses and his answer to practically everything and his confidence that I could be a carbon copy of dear old dead old dad. But there's not many other people to talk to.

I had a shock last night. Late on, me and Rick, who was on night duty, were watching TV. A night-time rock show, new talent spot. To tell you the truth, I'd all but fallen asleep, when Rick said something about a girl on TV. Typical Rick.

Lisa. No doubt about it. Lisa and I *think* one or two of the EMs, but mainly a new band. Lisa, singing to me and Rick. A song called "Lonely Spaceman". I like it. It's a good song, Lisa. I wonder if Ed knows about her new career. Rick didn't seem to recognize her, but why should he?

Next week, Stanley is taking me to Beckford, then I'm going with Mum and Mike and probably Stanley to buy a new suit for the wedding. My first outing, it's all arranged. I'm supposed to be nervous about it. I was nervous about it before. Now I should be more nervous, although funnily enough I'm not. Now I know why I'm going. I don't think it'll be too hard getting past Stanley. I hope Lisa likes the suit.